MUMMY DEAREST . . .

A door creaked. Harry reached under his coat, drew his Colt .38. Through the archway, a linen-wrapped figure came limping. It looked like a mummy, with its head wizened and nearly skeletal. One arm hung stiff at the figure's side, and its limp grew more pronounced as it took a few more faltering steps into the Antiquités Égyptiennes Wing.

"Flee, O despoiler of tombs," the mummy intoned.

Harry grinned. "If you're already dead, friend, a bullet won't bother you," he told the mummy.

The creature took one more faltering step. "Huh . . . just a moment, monsieur . . ."

Worlds of Fantasy from Avon Books

THE CHRONICLES OF THE TWELVE KINGDOMS
by Esther M. Friesner
MUSTAPHA AND HIS WISE DOG
SPELLS OF MORTAL WEAVING
THE WITCHWOOD CRADLE

THE DUCHESS OF KNEEDEEP
by Atanielle Annyn Noël

FANTASISTS ON FANTASY
edited by Robert H. Boyer and Kenneth J. Zahorski

MURDER ON USHER'S PLANET
by Atanielle Annyn Noël

100 GREAT FANTASY SHORT SHORT STORIES
edited by Isaac Asimov, Terry Carr, and Martin H. Greenberg

THE PIG, THE PRINCE & THE UNICORN
by Karen A. Brush

TALKING MAN
by Terry Bisson

UNICORN & DRAGON
(trade paperback)
by Lynn Abbey

VALE OF THE VOLE
by Piers Anthony

WINDMASTER'S BANE
by Tom Deitz

WOLF-DREAMS
by Michael D. Weaver

Coming Soon

THE BLIND ARCHER
by John Gregory Betancourt

THE CRYSTAL SWORD
by Adrienne Martine-Barnes

FIRESHAPER'S DOOM
by Tom Deitz

THE CURSE
OF
THE OBELISK

RON GOULART

AVON
PUBLISHERS OF BARD, CAMELOT, DISCUS AND FLARE BOOKS

THE CURSE OF THE OBELISK is an original publication of Avon Books. This work has never before appeared in book form. This work is a novel. Any similarity to actual persons or events is purely coincidental.

AVON BOOKS
A division of
The Hearst Corporation
105 Madison Avenue
New York, New York 10016

Copyright © 1987 by Ron Goulart
Front cover illustration by James Warhola
Published by arrangement with the author
Library of Congress Catalog Card Number: 87-91591
ISBN: 0-380-89858-6

First Avon Printing: November 1987

AVON TRADEMARK REG. U.S. PAT. OFF. AND IN OTHER COUNTRIES, MARCA REGISTRADA, HECHO EN U.S.A.

Printed in the U.S.A.

K-R 10 9 8 7 6 5 4 3 2 1

Chapter 1

Paris in the spring of 1897 was a city of gaiety, light and movement, pervaded with an air of joyous living. An immense city, full of broad handsome streets, magnificent buildings, grand open spaces with fountains and statues, great public gardens and parks, miles and miles of stores and shops filled with the most beautiful and interesting things that are made or found in any part of the world.

Harry Challenge didn't much want to be there.

As he went striding along the twilight Boulevard Saint Germain, unlit cigar clenched in his teeth, he made a list of places he'd rather be.

A lean man of middle height, Harry was dark haired and clean shaven. His tan, weather-beaten face tended to give people the impression he was a few years older than his thirty-one years. He wore, as he usually did, a dark suit. His hat was soft brimmed, and in his snug shoulder holster rested a Colt .38 revolver.

"Fool's errand," Harry muttered to himself. Not for the first time.

An open carriage rolled by, the horses' hooves clacking on the smooth pavement. The satin-clad woman in the carriage glanced approvingly at Harry, and the light of a street lamp made the diamonds in her tiara and on the collar of her little white Maltese dog sparkle. Scowling, the dog yapped at Harry.

He tipped his hat to both of them and hurried on.

The street was crowded. People strolling, people sitting at the little tables in front of cafés, workmen in blue blouses and wooden shoes heading homeward, even a priest in long black clothes and a broad felt hat taking the air.

Absently Harry patted the pocket of his vest that contained a folded copy of the latest cable from his father in New York. The message had been waiting for him when he checked into his far too fancy Paris hotel this afternoon. What it said was:

> *Dear son: Get off your rump. Go see our half-wit client. Name is Maurice Allegre. He runs the Musée des Antiquités on Rue Balbec. If you ask me he's got bats in his bonnet, but his money's good. You find out what's really going on. I doubt his museum is haunted. Your loving father, the Challenge International Detective Agency.*

An earlier message, which had reached Harry while he was finishing up a case in the capital city of the small sovereign nation of Orlandia had mentioned a mummy that roamed the museum by night.

Harry'd handled several supernatural cases of late, too many in fact, and he was hoping M. Allegre would turn out to be, as his father implied, suffering from hallucinations.

He passed the Café de Flor, dropped a few centimes in the dented copper cup of the ragged blind man standing just beyond its bright Art Nouveau facade and turned onto the Rue Balbec.

The dusk was deepening. From a sharply slanting tile roof a clutter of sparrows rose up into the oncoming night. Someone was playing a mournful tune on a rusty violin in a lamplit parlor up in a thin building on his left.

Cutting across the cobblestoned street, Harry started

through a public garden. A greened brass plate on the stone column at its entrance proclaimed it the Jardin Rêve.

According to his red-bound Baedeker, the museum he sought was on the opposite side of this shadowy, block-square little park.

The light was fading faster. Darkness and quiet came closing in on Harry. He seemed to be the only person walking through the Jardin Rêve. Yet Harry was commencing to feel a shade uneasy, wondering if he really wasn't alone.

The white gravel path wound through a thick grove of trees. In among them lurked pale white figures that Harry decided, after reaching into his coat for his .38 revolver and then thinking better of it, were statues.

He recognized, quickening his pace, a pudgy Venus and a muscle-bound Hercules.

Through the dark trees ahead he spotted now the two glowing electric lamps that framed the arched doorway of the Musée des Antiquités.

From behind him came a rustling sound.

Halting, he spun around. He drew his Colt and stared into the darkness behind him.

Harry had the impression something large and dark had settled into the high branches of one of the big trees a few hundred yards away.

He stood still, eyes narrowed and gun ready, watching.

The shape he thought he'd noticed wasn't there. Or if it was, the new night masked it.

He waited nearly a full minute before holstering his gun and continuing on his way.

Not quite ten seconds after that a young woman screamed. Two pistol shots rang out.

Harry dived to the ground, rolled across the grass and came to a squatting position behind a wide tree trunk. His Colt was once again in his right hand.

"Well, damn," he remarked aloud.

Rising up above the treetops was an immense birdlike

creature. Its body was nearly man-size and it had bat wings that creaked and made bellows sounds as it flapped them.

Harry sprinted back to the gravel path for a better look.

Down out of the night sky fell a drop of something hot and sticky. It splashed him on the cheek.

"Serves me right." He yanked out his pocket handkerchief, wiped at his face and stuffed the cloth away.

The giant bird or bat or whatever it was was flying away over the rooftops of Paris. The glow of street lamps and window lights illuminated it until the creature rose too high. Darkness swallowed it.

Putting away his gun, Harry went trotting back the way he'd come. "Now where the hell's the lady who hollered?"

She was slumped on a wrought iron bench, a derringer lying in the grass at her feet. A slim and very pretty young woman she was, her hair a pale reddish gold. It had tumbled down from under the checkered cap she was wearing. The cap matched the man's Norfolk jacket and tweedy knickers she had herself decked out in.

"Jennie Barr." Harry's tone was not especially cordial. "You were too busy to have dinner with me tonight. You had to get to work immediately on your story for the New York *Daily Inquirer*. You lied to me."

Taking a deep breath, Jennie sat up straighter and tucked her hair back up under the cap. "Well, I suppose I did fib some, yes."

"We travel all the way from Zevenburg to Paris together," he continued, angry. "I even, behaving like what my father would classify as a nincompoop, declare that I'm fond of you. I entertain the half-wit notion that I can trust you not to be a newspaper reporter above all else. But you were just conning me, Jennie, so you could—"

"Fond of me? What you did on the Zevenburg-Paris Express, Harry, was tell me you loved me."

"Okay, I do love you," he admitted. "Fact is, I was in the process of telling you that again just a few hours ago.

But you told me you had to get right to work on your assignment. No time for romance, no time for the gaiety, light and movement of Paris. So it turns out this damn story of yours has to do with my private—''

"Hey, I just saved your life."

"Thanks," he said. "Now tell me why you're dressed like a guy and tailing me."

Jennie grinned. "Did pretty darn well, didn't I? I followed you all the way from the Hotel Grand-Luxe and you never even tumbled."

"You did, huh?" He made a face and shook his head. "There's one thing my father's right about. Getting involved with a woman dulls your—''

"Your father, if you'll forgive my reminding you of the fact, is a sour ball, Harry," the reporter put in. "One of the things that scares the heck out of me is the possibility you'll grow more like him as you get older. Spending my declining years with a curmudgeon isn't my idea of—''

"You won't even spend the rest of the damn evening with me unless you explain what's going on."

Reaching up, she took hold of his arm and pulled herself to her feet. "Take me to a nearby café and over coffee I'll tell all," Jennie promised.

"I'm on my way to see a client. Don't have time for—''

"Let me give you some advice." She bent, grimacing, scooped up her tiny gun and tucked it away under her jacket. "Don't pout that way. You don't have the face for it. I think it's an attractive face, albeit a mite beat-up and—''

"Okay, I'll take you someplace." When they started to walk, he noticed the red-haired young woman was limping. "Did that critter hurt you?"

"Nope, but I twisted my ankle while I was running and shooting at it. That's why I fell and dropped my gun."

"You can't faze a gigantic bird with a dinky gun like that anyway."

"Wasn't a gigantic bird," she assured Harry. "It was a gigantic bat."

                        *   *   *

Jennie poked at her raspberry ice with her spoon. "It is, you have to admit, the sort of story I do well." She'd taken off the cap and the faint night breeze brushed at her hair.

Across the small outdoor table from her Harry lit his cigar. "A curse?" He blew smoke at the marble tabletop.

"Three weeks ago the noted French archaeologist Reynard Courdaud met a strange end at his villa near Nice," said the reporter. "Then five days ago Sir Munson Bellhouse died in a fall while hunting in Scotland."

"A death in Nice, another in Scotland. Why does that prompt the *Daily Inquirer* to send you here to Paris?"

After savoring a spoonful of the ice, she answered, "You haven't done, Harry, sufficient research into this affair."

The light spilling out through the stained glass window of the sidewalk café gave a pale golden glow to her face. Harry looked away for a moment, toward a plump German tourist who was sipping a solitary absinthe. "Was Bellhouse an archaeologist, too?"

Jennie nodded. "He was one of the five men who headed the expedition to the Valley of Jackals in 1895," she said. "They found considerable treasures, including the dornick that's been dubbed the Osiris Obelisk."

"Is it anything like the one in Central Park or the one right here in town at the Place de la Concorde?"

"This is a miniature version, only about six feet high. Thing is, one of the inscriptions started the rumor that—"

"Wait now. Is there a curse on the thing?"

"There was a lot of talk to that effect, back when the Courdaud expedition first broke into the tomb it was standing in front of. My editors believe there's a—"

"Awful slow for a curse. Don't they work faster than that?" He rested his elbows on the tabletop, watching her faintly freckled face. "Waiting two years before striking isn't my idea of—"

"Let me give you a few details about Reynard Courdaud's death." She set her spoon aside. "His valet swears that Courdaud was attacked on his terrace at dusk by a giant bat. That's one reason I hollered and started shooting when I saw that thing tonight lurking over your—"

"A giant bat?" Harry sat up.

"Your elbow." Jennie pointed. "You've got something sticky on it."

"Coffee." Fishing out his handkerchief, he wiped at his coat. "This seems to be my night for . . . hum."

"What is it?"

He'd brought the stained square of linen up to his nose and was sniffing at it. "While I'm not an expert on bat lore, I'll bet their droppings don't smell like machine oil."

She reached across and took the handkerchief. "That's oil sure enough. What makes you think—"

"While that thing was flying away directly overhead, I looked up."

Crumpling the handkerchief, Jennie said, "This is commencing to look like one of the oddest curses I've ever investigated."

"This guy in Scotland . . ."

"Sir Munson Bellhouse, one of the most respected archaeologists in Britain. Haven't you ever heard of—"

"What caused his fall?"

"A gamekeeper from the estate where they were shooting swore he saw a giant bird circling the spot where Sir Munson did his brodie. He wasn't believed."

"Okay, and where do I tie in?" asked Harry. "Was that damn bat planning to make me the next victim of the curse of the obelisk? And if so, why?"

"Don't you know where the Osiris Obelisk is?"

Harry ground his cigar out in the pewter ashtray. "At the Musée des Antiquités?"

"For five more days," she replied. "Then it's being shipped to the capital of Urbania. The museum's sold it to a private collector. The whole business has caused quite a stir.''

Harry said, ''You were trailing me because you figure the troubles at the museum are linked with this curse.''

''Seems likely, doesn't it?'' There was a mixture of contriteness and excitement in her voice. ''Honestly, Harry, I don't like to trade on our friendship, but so far nobody else knows the Challenge International Detective Agency has been called in on this case. That exclusive angle'll make my series of articles for the *Daily Inquirer* much more—''

''I'll make you a deal.''

''You sound sort of grim.''

''Instead of putting on half-wit disguises and skulking around, you can come along to the museum with me,'' he said. ''After I meet with M. Allegre, in private, I'll see if he'll let you interview him.''

''Well, that'd be fine, I guess. But you're scowling at me as though—''

''We've known each other for quite a spell. Back in New York and—''

''Known *and* liked. Even though sometimes—''

''When our paths crossed in Orlandia and it turned out we were both interested in the prisoner of Blackwood Castle, I initially tried to ditch you.''

''Harry, I do . . . well, love you. And you can trust me,'' she assured him in a quiet voice. ''It's just that I'm a reporter, and a darn good one, and so sometimes—''

''We'll forget what happened on the train from Orlandia to Paris.'' Harry stood and signaled the gaunt, aproned waiter. ''It never took place. We'll go back to being rivals, friendly rivals.''

''But, Harry, something did happen. We can't just—''

''I'm late for the meeting with my client. You coming along?''

She hesitated, then smiled tentatively. ''Yes,'' she replied.

Chapter 2

After rubbing at his nose, Maurice Allegre tapped the drawing in the newspaper open upon his desk. "My reputation is in shreds already, M. Challenge," he said, wringing his small hands. "Just this past Monday here in *Le Figaro* no less a formidable penman than Caran d'Ache depicted me as a grave robber. You see?"

Harry leaned forward in his heavy wooden chair. "Doesn't resemble you that much."

"Ah, but all Paris knows at whom this barb is aimed," said the forlorn museum director. "Even though he's seen fit to give me an extremely large Hebraic nose. It is sad enough to be blamed for selling that accursed obelisk without being branded a Dreyfusard as well. If the outside world were to learn of my latest sorrows . . ." He sighed.

"Suppose you detail your problem to me."

The office was shadowy, the furniture heavy and dark, the carpets and drapes the color of deep autumn. Hovering in the dim corners that the light from the faintly hissing gas lamps didn't reach were coffins, mummy cases and at least one suit of Oriental armor.

Allegre patted at the part in his slick dark hair. "My two regular watchmen had let me down," he said, taking another disheartened glance at the cartoon attacking him. "After all, M. Challenge, I do not own this Musée des Antiquités. Nay, I am but an employee. When the directors, you understand, agreed to sell the obelisk to Baron Groll in Urbania, I could only, meekly, go along with them.'' He poked a delicate finger at the cartoon. ''This is, after all, a private institution and not a public one. They can sell whatever they wish and to whomsoever they wish. Therefore, when this Caran d'Ache shows me looting tombs and selling the treasures of France to foreigners, he errs in—''

''You told my father your museum was haunted.''

Allegre said, ''Your father, at least in his cablegrams, strikes one as a highly intelligent man. I was halfway expecting that he himself would journey here to Paris to handle the—''

''He rarely travels these days,'' said Harry. ''Do you have ghosts?''

Allegre shrugged with both his shoulders and both hands. ''Ah, but I myself have seen not a one,'' he replied. ''My addlepated watchmen, on the other hand, insist that on several occasions some unusual incidents have taken place.''

''Such as?''

''Most, if not all, of this outré activity has allegedly occurred in our Antiquités Égyptiennes Wing, M. Challenge,'' said the director. ''Both Gaspar and Albert have insisted they heard many strange sounds and, furthermore, that they saw with their own eyes . . .'' He shrugged once again. ''They saw one of the mummified corpses leave its resting place and walk.''

''When did these incidents begin?''

Allegre answered, ''Approximately three weeks ago. Fortunately, I have been able, thus far, to keep it quiet. I fear that—''

''I'd like to talk to Gaspar and Albert.''

''Ah, but alas, monsieur, that is not possible,'' explained Allegre. ''They are no longer employed here. Albert, in point of fact, ran screaming from this place three midnights ago. Though Gaspar made a less flamboyant exit, he too is gone.''

"Is midnight when the ghostly happenings usually happen?"

"Not every midnight, but far too many, yes," answered the museum director. "You also cannot, I fear, interrogate either Gerard or Paul."

"The new watchmen?"

"Exactly, monsieur." He sighed his deepest sigh thus far. "Gerard and Paul lasted but a single night. Thus, you have indeed arrived at a most fortunate juncture in the affairs of our plagued institution."

Harry eyed him for a few sconds. "You want me to act as watchman tonight?"

"Are you not ideally suited for such a task? A stalwart and manly fellow, well versed in the handling of such unusual situations," said Allegre. "You know how to deport yourself when faced with dangers of an unusual sort, and you are not superstitious like Gaspar, Albert, Gerard and Paul."

"Have you ever spent a night here?"

The director shuddered. "I am, you understand, not a brave man," he confided. "Were I to run screaming from the premises in the dead of night it might lead to further scandal, providing fodder for yet another unflattering caricature in *Le Figaro* and other vicious publications. Besides, M. Challenge, since we are paying you such an enormous fee, it is only fair that—"

"Substantial," corrected Harry, "not enormous. Okay, I'll stay here tonight. That'll me a chance to go over the Egyptian wing and the rest of the museum."

"I appreciate that," said Allegre, allowing himself a small, sad smile. "Will your quite charming young assistant who waits in the foyer be sharing your nocturnal duties, monsieur?"

Harry grinned. "Yes, I seldom go anywhere without her."

*   *   *

The ceiling of the vast room was lost in shadows. The air was chill, scented faintly with sandalwood and ancient dust.

"This particular chest is one of my favorites," Allegre was saying. "The framework is of ebony, the inner panels of beautifully carved redwood. Here we see the bronze and ivory blended to produce . . ."

Jennie whispered to Harry, "You're a rat."

He assumed a beatific expression and ignored her.

"Passing me off as an operative in your dim-witted detective agency after promising me a chance to interview this guy." She delivered a disappointed nudge to his ribs.

"He loathes the press. Now hush."

". . . the king, you see, is offering Omnophris a pot of perfume and a lamp. Omnophris is, of course, but another guise of Osiris, who guards the . . ."

"I'm not some pushy French news hound," persisted Jennie in an annoyed whisper. "And if you don't tell him who I really am, then I myself will."

"Listen, didn't I arrange for you to spend the whole damn night inside this place? When the mummy does his jig, you'll be the only reporter on hand."

"Yes, but—"

"You go telling him who you really are and you'll get nothing but the old heave-ho."

"Ah, but I must be boring you by riding my hobbyhorse so vehemently." The director turned away from the glass case that housed the chest.

"I'd like to see the case the mummy climbs out of at midnight," Harry told him.

"But certainly, monsieur." Bowing slightly, Allegre led them past more ornate chests, an alabaster casket, a case filled with glittering bracelets and bangles.

In an alcove, illuminated by a single hanging lamp, a carved coffin with a lid of gold, turquoise and crimson rested on a low platform.

Noticing something stuck to a nail on the platform,

Harry bent and took it. "Little hunk of linen," he said, passing it under his nose. "Doesn't smell especially ancient."

The museum director blinked. "May I inspect that, monsieur?"

"I don't think it came from the mummy in that case."

"No, certainly not. This bit of cloth is of recent manufacture." He was rubbing it between his fingers. "Superficially like that used to wrap the bodies of our Egyptian friends, yet not the real thing. How, do you think, did this come to be here?"

Retrieving the patch, Harry tucked it into the watch pocket of his vest. "We'll try to find that out tonight."

Allegre gestured at the coffin. "This is made of wood. Over the lid was placed first a layer of plaster and then one of gold. After which the—"

"Does the lid lift off easily?" inquired Jennie.

"It is not too difficult to remove, Mlle. Barr." Smiling, he demonstrated.

Harry took a look inside. "This fellow can't do much walking around, not with his legs wrapped together that way."

"Precisely what I tried to explain to those fools, Gaspar and Albert." He nodded toward Jennie. "Would you care for a glimpse of King Baydmadroub II?"

"Pass," she said.

"Now I'd like," requested Harry, "to see the obelisk."

After returning the inlaid coffin lid to its place, Allegre said, "It's really not that impressive, monsieur. A very small and stunted thing that is no match for the so-called Cleopatra's Needle that—"

"Even so."

The director sighed, shrugged, patted his hair. "Very well. If you will but follow me."

Slowly he led them through the big room, along a dimly lit corridor and into a smaller room.

Mounted upright on a wooden stand was the miniature

obelisk, a tapering shaft of red granite profusely covered with carved hieroglyphs. Two small gas lamps, one on each side of the room, provided the only light.

Allegre hunched his shoulders. "A paltry example, hardly worth making a fuss about," he observed, stroking his nose. "It stands approximately six foot eight in height, which makes it roughly one tenth the size of the obelisk to be found in your country."

Jennie edged closer. "Do these inscriptions spell out the curse?"

"Among other things." Reluctantly he joined her near the obelisk. "Those lower rows there, near the base, provide the phrases that give the obelisk its unsavory reputation."

Harry strolled over. "What do they say exactly?"

Impatiently Allegre translated. " 'By the awesome power of Osiris, who holds the secret of eternal life, cursed be those who disturb this tomb. Death, not life, shall be their sure and swift reward.' And so forth and so on. A standard and not especially imaginative curse, as ancient curses go. Yet sufficient, because of the idiocies practiced by the disgraceful press to—"

"Some reporters," put forth Jennie, "are highly reputable."

"I am astounded to hear you express such sentiments, Mlle. Barr, since America's newspapers are, one is told, even more vile than—"

"Is Osiris usually associated with the secret of eternal life?" asked Harry.

"He is the king and the judge of the dead," answered Allegre. "One doesn't often find him addressed in exactly these terms, yet the association is—"

"Take the New York *Daily Inquirer*. There's an honest and well written paper," said Jennie. "Why, some of the reporters on its staff are—"

"We'd best get on with your inspection tour, Operative Barr." Harry slipped an arm around her slim waist and gave her an unobtrusive prod in the ribs. "You and M.

Allegre can chat about journalism some other time. I want
to check all the entrances before he leaves us.''

"Ah, yes," said the director after consulting his gold
pocket watch, "the hour does indeed grow late. I would
like to be far from here before midnight strikes." He
started out of the room.

After kicking Harry in the shin, Jennie followed.

Chapter 3

Jennie placed the tray on the floor near a case that held a gilded leopard mask. "The coffee isn't too bad," she said, sitting down cross-legged on a sofa cushion she'd appropriated from the long departed director's office, "considering I had to brew it over a spirit lamp. Have some, it'll keep you awake."

"I am awake." He was hunkered on the floor of the Egyptian wing, back against the buff wall. "Never go to sleep on a job."

"I thought that was the Pinkerton slogan." She passed him a delicate china cup. "The petits fours I can't vouch for. They may be a mite stale since I found them in a tin in a bottom drawer of his desk."

Harry sipped the coffee and declined the tiny cakes.

"What about that little piece of cloth you found?" she asked him. "You got a whiff of something off it."

"Greasepaint."

"That must mean—"

"Could mean several things." He looked away from her, toward the corridor leading to the obelisk.

After a moment Jennie asked, "Are you still miffed at me?"

"Miffed isn't exactly the word I'd use."

Out in the Paris night a bell began to toll midnight.

Jennie tried one of the petits fours, wrinkled her nose,

then went on chewing. "You still don't realize, Harry, how difficult it is for me to balance things. My career requires my traveling all over the world for stories and that means I can't have a settled way of life. I have a sort of rule not to let myself get too involved with anybody anywhere. But then I bumped into you again and . . . well, it makes things rough."

"I know, torn between love and duty," he said. "Saw a heartrending painting on the subject once in a saloon in Elko, Nevada."

She gave him a polite snort. "Mother O'Malley! You're the most—"

"Quiet a minute." He put a hand on her arm.

"You hear something?"

Slowly and silently Harry eased to his feet. "Key turning in a lock somewhere."

The auburn-haired reporter stood, watchful and listening.

A door creaked. The sound came drifting to them across the big, chill room.

Harry reached under his coat. "Get back against the wall."

"I want to see what's—"

"Back." He pushed her into the shadows.

Moving away from Jennie, he started for an arched doorway.

"Beware," moaned an echoing voice, "the graves of the sacred dead had been defiled."

Harry drew his Colt .38. "Speaks pretty fair French for an Egyptian ghost."

"Be careful, Harry."

Through the archway a linen-wrapped figure came limping. It looked somewhat like a mummy, with its head wizened and nearly skeletal. One arm hung stiff at the figure's side and its limp grew more pronounced as it took a few more faltering steps into the Antiquités Égyptiennes Wing.

"Flee, O despoiler of tombs," the mummy intoned.

Harry grinned. "If you're already dead, friend, a bullet won't bother you," he told the mummy. "But if you're some down-and-out actor dressed up to throw a scare into us, then you'll be joining the sacred dead right soon."

The creature took one more faltering step. "A moment, monsieur," it said. "You are obviously more sophisticated than the other watchmen. Therefore, let me suggest a—"

"Not open to suggestions," Harry told him. "Raise your hands up high and then walk over here."

"There's no reason why we can't agree on—"

Two shots sounded. They both hit the mummy in the chest. It brought up a bandage-wrapped hand to clutch at the bloody spots that were swiftly spreading.

"But, monsieur, I thought we . . ."

Its left knee hit the floor, then the other. There was blood staining the bandages all down the torso. Gasping, swaying, the mummy suddenly died. It fell over on its ancient face, twitching.

In the corridor it had emerged from there was the sound of at least two pairs of booted feet running. A door opened, then slammed.

Harry didn't give chase. Nor did he cross to the dead man.

He turned, his gun still in his hand, to stare at Jennie. "Why the hell did you shoot him?" he asked her.

The young woman's face had gone pale, the freckles stood out. She was shivering hard, teeth chattering. Her frightened eyes went from Harry to the derringer in her hand and back to Harry. "I don't know," she said. "I don't know."

Harry turned up the flame on the wall gas lamp. "Feeling better?"

"Not especially, no." Jennie, hugging herself and still shivering slightly, was sitting in an armchair in the museum foyer.

"Fairly soon now I'm going to have to telephone the

police," he said. "We ought to be able to convince them it's self-defense. But just for myself, I'd like to know why you killed the guy."

She shook her head sadly. "I really don't have any idea, Harry."

"Maybe you were rattled. You assumed the mummy was going to attack me and—"

"C'mon, I don't rattle under pressure. You know darn well I can keep my nerve under just about any circumstances," she said. "If I could stand being locked up for a week on Blackwell's Island for a story or face an escaped lunatic in the wilds of— "

"Okay, I was just trying to suggest a reason."

"I don't have one," Jennie said. "I was as anxious as you were to get him to talk. An exclusive interview with a mummy, even a fake one, would've been marvelous for my newspaper story. All of a sudden, though, I had this overwhelming impulse to gun him down."

Harry rested a hip on the arm of her tufted chair and touched her shoulder. "Like a cup of coffee?"

"Hemlock would be more—"

An exuberant knocking had begun on the street door of the museum.

Standing, Harry said, "Can't be the police."

"What ho within!" boomed a deep voice.

Jennie brightened. "That sounds like—"

"The Great Lorenzo." Harry sprinted across the thick Oriental carpeting, unlocked the heavy oaken door and yanked it open.

The portly magician stepped in out of the night. He was clad in a suit of evening clothes, a jauntily tilted top hat and a flowing, scarlet-lined cloak. The buttons of his silky waistcoat glittered almost as brightly as real diamonds. "Ah, you're not dead, my boy." He chuckled with relief and gave his greying muttonchop whiskers a fluff.

"Was I supposed to be?"

The Great Lorenzo noticed Jennie, who was standing

beside the maroon armchair. Doffing his hat, he bowed in her direction. "Good evening, young lady," he said. "You don't look as pert as when last we met in Orlandia."

Harry shut the door. "You were supposed to be en route to Urbania by now, you and your entire magic show."

"Indeed I was." He placed his topper on a claw-footed table. "You and I, Harry, have been chums for lo! these many years. I, modestly, tend to think of myself as a second father to—"

"I like you better than that."

"Ah, yes, I forgot for the moment that your dear papa lacks many of the warm and lovable traits that I am blessed with." He fluffed his ample sideburns once again. "As I was saying, dear lad, I have never professed to be anything more than a humble stage illusionist—the best professional magician in the world if one believes the critics and an idolatrous and adoring public—simply a man with nary a true supernatural gift. And yet . . ."

"You had one of your visions?"

He was gazing across the foyer at Jennie. "You're extremely peeked, my child," he observed. "What was I saying, Harry?"

"You had another of your mystical hunches."

"Indeed I did." He rubbed at his broad chest. "Most inconvenient it was, too, striking as it did whilst I happened to be sharing the opulently furnished private railroad car of an impressively amorous countess and demonstrating my fabled manual dexterity." He paused to cough into his gloved hand. "Of a sudden I was taken over with a most unsettling vision, my boy. What I saw was none other than yourself stretched out in what appeared to be a gaudy Egyptian sarcophagus, all swaddled with linen wrappings. The wrappings in question were splattered with blood and you, alas, appeared to be singularly defunct."

"As sometimes happens, Lorenzo, you got your facts slightly garbled. But even so I—"

"This strange and awesome power, if indeed I do possess it—and I make no claims—doesn't always work with the accuracy and dependability of the telegraph,'' said the plump magician. ''Included in the trance image was the address of this benighted institution, today's date and the warning that the traditional hour of midnight was the crucial one. I made arrangements to disembark from the Orlandia-Urbania Express and hastened here. An unfortunate altercation with my cabdriver over the sanitary habits of one of his steeds caused me to arrive a few moments beyond the witching hour. Yet I am pleased to observe that no serious harm has as yet befallen anyone.''

Harry took hold of his plump arm. ''Step into the Egyptian wing,'' he invited. ''Will you be okay for a few minutes, Jennie?''

''As well as can be expected.'' She sank back into the chair.

Frowning, the magician allowed Harry to escort him down a corridor and into the large room where the dead man was sprawled. ''Ah, there is an approximation of the very bloody corpse I saw in my vision. Except it isn't you, Harry.''

''This guy's been sneaking in here evenings to scare off the watchmen.''

Puffing some and grunting, the Great Lorenzo knelt beside the mummy. ''What precisely was his motivation?''

''Never had the chance to ask him.''

''You were forced to shoot him to prevent his doing you and the fair Jennie bodily harm, eh? Well, that's understand—''

''Jennie shot him.''

The magician's knees made small crackling noises as he got up. ''I fail to detect a note of gratitude.''

''He was about to give himself up.''

The Great Lorenzo made a slow thoughtful circuit of the body. ''There's something familiar about this lad,'' he muttered.

''Know him?''

"Not as a bosom friend, no. Yet I have the feeling I've encountered him sometime in the past," he replied. "Most likely during one of my many triumphal engagements here in this dazzling and wordly city."

"Somebody connected with the theater maybe."

"Yes, that sounds . . ." The magician grimaced suddenly, clutched at his middle.

"What's wrong?"

"Jennie." He pivoted, starting trotting toward the foyer.

Harry ran faster, reaching the young woman ahead of the magician. "You seem to be all right," he told her, puzzled.

"No worse that I was a few minutes ago when you dragged Lorenzo off to view my handiwork." She was looking up into his face. "What were you expecting to find?"

"He gave me the impression you were in danger."

"She is, my boy." Panting, the Great Lorenzo halted beside the tufted armchair.

"From the police you mean?"

He bent and took both her hands in his. "Sometime within the last dozen hours, dear child," he informed her, "you were hypnotized. And for an evil purpose."

"By whom?" asked Harry.

"Alas, my latest vision failed to include that helpful kernel of information."

Chapter 4

The sky began to lighten. In the thin blueness of dawn Harry saw the Eiffel Tower take shape in the distance, a dark skeleton rising up into the pale morning.

He turned away from the paneled windows of his hotel suite parlor. The room was mostly shades of brown, with touches of mauve and gold.

Seated comfortably on a candy-striped loveseat was the Great Lorenzo. He'd removed his gloves and was fingering a large silver coin. "The procedure, I assure you, is completely and utterly painless."

Jennie, who was now wearing a full-length dark skirt and a puff-sleeved white blouse, was pacing the ochre and mauve carpet. "Well, it'll be just about the first thing that is since I hit Paris this morning."

Harry stationed himself in front of a wall covered with vertically striped purple and chocolate wallpaper. "You don't remember running into anyone unusual after you ditched me in the lobby?"

"I didn't exactly ditch you," she said. "I really was sent here to cover this obelisk story, though. Those cablegrams I showed Inspector Swann prove that. . . . Thanks, by the way, Harry, for vouching for me and telling the police I was more or less assisting you on this case."

"Swann knows my father and, for some reason, admires him," said Harry. "So he seems to have nothing but

respect for the Challenge International Detective Agency
and all its investigators.''

"Your papa," remarked the Great Lorenzo, "may be a
cantankerous old goat, yet he's a sterling sleuth for all
that. You're perhaps too young to recall in full the details
of such cases of his as the affair of the Yonkers Trunk
Slayer back in '77 or—''

"Can you counteract whatever's been done to Jennie?''

The coin was spinning from plump finger to plump
finger, catching the light of the electric chandelier overhead. "A trifling task, my boy. Fear not.''

Jennie took a slow deep breath, then exhaled. "Well,
let's get started.''

The portly magician gestured at the lyre-backed wooden
chair near the small empty fireplace. "If you will but seat
yourself, dear child.''

Jennie complied. "I think, Harry, I really was planning
to follow you on the sly," Jennie confessed as she smoothed
her skirt. "But, honestly, I'm not even sure of that.''

"Don't fret. Lorenzo'll get you back shipshape.''

"This is a silver dollar," the magician told her. "On
one side we notice Liberty and on the other an eagle.
Watch now . . . Liberty . . . eagle . . . Liberty . . .
eagle . . .''

Her hazel eyes were already taking on a glazed look.

"The eagle seems to be . . . flapping his wings . . .
flapping them . . . not rapidly . . . but slowly . . .
slowly . . .''

Jennie made a small whimpering sound and slumped
sideways in her chair.

Harry moved to help her up, but the Great Lorenzo
waved him off.

"You're asleep now, dear child," the magician informed her. "A very pleasant sleep, very relaxing. You
can hear me as you blissfully slumber and, what is more,
you will be able to speak. Isn't that right?''

"It is, yes." Her voice was faint and childlike.

"Not a thing can hurt you, nothing can harm you," the Great Lorenzo assured her. "No matter what you have been told earlier. Is that clear?"

Her hands clenched into fists. "Yes . . ."

"Sometime today, after you arrived in Paris, you were hypnotized. Is that so?"

She shuddered. "I must not . . . ever say . . ."

"No, no, child. You simply misunderstood the original instructions. I am in control now. The Great Lorenzo is in charge and what I tell you, and only that, is true."

The shuddering grew more severe. Jennie shut her eyes tight, hitting her fists together. "If I ever speak . . . terrible things . . ."

"That was an error. A false bit of news sent to you. I am the only one you need listen to. The Great Lorenzo. Listen to me now, Jennie, listen. Whatever was told to you by another hypnotist, whatever warnings you were given, whatever orders . . . they are no more. Your mind is yours again; it belongs to none other. And you will remember all that happened."

She shivered even more violently. "But I must obey . . . the . . ." Leaping to her feet, she held her arms out and cried, "Harry, Harry! Help me."

He bounded to her, put his arms around her. "Easy now. It's all right."

She hugged him hard, beginning to sob against his chest. "It was like . . . like being attacked by . . . Oh, Harry, just hold on to me. Please."

The Great Lorenzo flipped the silver dollar into the air. It vanished up near the cocoa ceiling. "I suggest we adjourn for a bit of breakfast before delving into the question of the identity of the scoundrel who did this."

The restaurant's main dining room was covered over with a high dome of steel and glass. There was a flourishing potted palm next to their white-covered table and the Great Lorenzo, after brushing the last of the croissant

crumbs from his dimpled chin, plucked two lighted cigars
from it and passed one to Harry. "I am, dear friends, glad
I made this side trip to Paris," he told them, puffing
contentedly on his cigar. "I only regret I must journey
onward in but a few days in order to reach the fabled
Spielzeug Theater in Urbania's glittering capital in time for
the initial performance of my magical extravaganza."

"Damn good thing you did stop," Harry said. "Otherwise we wouldn't have known what had happened to
Jennie."

For the past several minutes Jennie had been writing in a
stenographer's notebook with a stub of a pencil. Sipping
now and then at her coffee, she paid no attention to Harry,
the Great Lorenzo or the other patrons in the as yet un-
crowded restaurant. "Well, I think I remember just about
everything now," she announced, dropping the pencil on
the crisp white tablecloth. "It's pretty darn strange . . .
and frightening."

Harry asked, "Are you up to talking about it?"

"Yes. Thanks to Lorenzo, I feel I've got my mind
back." She touched the magician's pudgy hand for an
instant, smiling at him. "You really are a wizard, you
know."

"I have never laid claim to any true magical powers,"
he reminded. "But one can't help but be aware that a few
of my little knacks do seem a trifle supernatural."

Jennie flipped back a few pages in her notebook. "You
have some serious opposition, Harry," she said. "Have
you ever heard of an Englishman named Max Orchardson?"

"A true mountebank," murmured the magician.

Harry exhaled smoke. "Sure, he's been called the most
decadent man in Europe," he said. "He supposedly pals
around with the *Yellow Book* crowd—Oscar Wilde, Au-
brey Beardsley and such—and also dabbles in black magic.
Though that last could be only an affectation."

"It isn't," she said. "I wrote a series of articles on
Orchardson last year while I was in London for my paper."

Harry frowned. "Don't recall seeing those."

"That's because they never ran," Jennie explained. "My editors decided we might be risking libel charges after . . . well, I'd had signed statements from several witnesses. One evening all of them suddenly burst into flames while sitting on my desk in the hotel room. Next, two of my best witnesses got in touch with me and claimed they'd lied. A third dived into the Thames one foggy night and never surfaced."

"Typical of the way Orchardson operates," commented the Great Lorenzo.

"The guy is really a magician?"

"The man seemingly does have true powers," he acknowledged. "He also has a great deal of money, earned in India long ago by kin less aesthetic than he. And, like Wilde, he is a master showman."

"I had a sworn account of devil worship and at least one instance of human sacrifice," said Jennie.

Harry asked her, "Is Orchardson here in Paris? Is he the one who hypnotized you?"

She nodded. "He was waiting in my hotel room," she said, shivering once. "He's an obese man, puffy and pale as death. He . . . even though I tried to fight against it . . . hypnotized me. Using an opal medallion he wears around his fat neck."

"Nowhere near as effective as a coin," said the magician.

"What were you supposed to do?"

She lowered her head, picked up the pencil and tapped at the tablecloth with its blunt tip. "Follow you, report to him all that you did while in Paris."

"He knows why I'm here?"

"Seemed to. At least he knew you were going to the museum and when. I was instructed to follow you."

"Why?"

"He's interested in the Osiris Obelisk."

Harry said, "What about shooting the mummy?"

She turned to the next page of the notes. "I was told to destroy anyone who tried to get near it."

"Including me?"

"No, no. I was only to keep close to you and report regularly to him."

"What about that giant bat?"

The Great Lorenzo coughed. "There's a striking detail no one has bothered to share with—"

"Fill you in later," Harry promised.

"I don't know anything about the bat," answered Jennie. "Apparently when I shot and scared the darn thing off, I was acting on my own."

"How were you supposed to report to Orchardson?"

"He's staying in a villa in a suburb of Paris, Neuilly-sur-Seine."

"When do you report?"

"Three this afternoon."

Harry nodded at the magician. "Is your afternoon free?"

"I had intended to rekindle a touching relationship with a countess who is, except for a cork leg, the quintessence of middle-aged charm and beauty," he replied. "However, I'll give up that pleasure to put myself entirely at your disposal, my boy."

"Good. We'll pay a call on Max Orchardson."

"Harry," warned Jennie, "he's dangerous."

"So am I."

Chapter 5

The Great Lorenzo swung his cane vigorously as he
hurried along the late morning sidewalk. He wore a suit of
an impressive green shade, an embroidered waistcoat and a
silk cravat whose bright color scheme rivaled that of a
rainbow. With his tongue placed behind his upper teeth, he
was whistling a music hall tune having to do with a
gentleman known as Burlington Bertie.

Dodging a family of strolling American tourists, he
turned down a side street off the Avenue Montaigne. The
shop he was seeking sat squeezed between a brownstone
office building and a dark-fronted bistro.

Inscribed in gilt on the narrow shop window was the
single name Grandville. Tumbled together on the other
side of the dusty glass were domino masks, curly blond
wigs, lace-trimmed fans, shaggy dark beards, straw hats
and pairs of tinted spectacles.

A tinny bell jangled when the magician pushed the dark
wood and stained glass door open. "You haven't changed
your window display since I was here last, Grandville,"
he announced to the long shadowy room. "My little lec-
ture on American methods of merchandising and advertis-
ing had no effect, alas."

Shelves lined the walls and were piled with hatboxes,
shoe boxes and bundles of clothes. Manikins dressed in the

costumes of other climes and other times stood patiently all around.

In a high-backed wicker chair at the rear of the long, narrow shop sat a small, dark man of fifty some years. He had both his hands resting on the ivory handle of a stout cane. "Ah, it has to be Lorenzo," he said, wheezing and struggling to his feet. "Who else speaks in a voice substantial enough to shatter glass."

"I hear there's a new tenor with the La Scala company whose vocal prowess comes near to equaling mine." The magician went striding toward the proprietor. "I trust I find you in good health, old friend."

Grandville's laugh was raspy and wheezy. "I am no worse," he replied. "But why are you in Paris, Lorenzo? I read you had been relegated to putting on your magic show in such backwaters as Zevenburg and Kaltzonburg."

"Old chum, I don't mind your addressing me as plain Lorenzo rather than the more acceptable Great Lorenzo," he informed him. "When you, however, allude to my world renowned festival of magical artistry as a mere magic show, I, sir, bristle."

Grandville laughed yet again. "You are appearing, then, in Paris?"

Leaning closer, the Great Lorenzo addressed the owner of the costume and makeup shop in a confiding tone. "I have taken time out from a very crowded schedule to put on a limited performance for a small, select audience."

"A command performance, eh?"

"One might say that, although I am not at liberty to divulge any details," he said. "In fact, I would appreciate it if you'd keep this visit of mine a secret."

"That should not be too difficult, for few of my friends or customers even know who you are," said Grandville. "Except for Goncourt the tailor who continues to complain that you owe him in the neighborhood of two hundred francs for some garments he ran up for you back in 1894 and for which you have not as—"

"Nonsense. I've never draped myself in his shabby work," the magician said. "Now, dear friend, let us return to the purpose of my call. I have need of two of your excellent costumes, plus the false whiskers and makeup that goes with them. One to fit my own manly frame, the other for a younger chap of medium height and more slender build."

Grandville rubbed thumb and forefinger together. "A cash deposit is required for all costume rentals, Lorenzo."

Giving him a disdainful look, the Great Lorenzo reached up into the musty air above the man's head and plucked a fistful of paper money. "Here, old friend. I trust this will soothe your greedy heart and allow us to—"

"This is German currency. Marks and—"

"Ah, forgive me, my mind is wandering." He grabbed the wad of bills back, crumpled it even further and flung it away from him. The bills vanished before reaching the dusty wooden floor. "I would like to see what you have in the way of costumes for—"

"My money."

"Eh?" The magician had wandered over to study one of the faded theatrical posters decorating the wall of the shop.

"The francs with which you intend to pay for the rental of the costumes and sundries you need."

Brow furrowed, the Great Lorenzo leaned to study the poster more closely. "Ah, that's the name I was trying to remember," he muttered. "The fellow wrapped in bandages last evening." He tapped the poster with a plump forefinger. "Whatever became of LePlaut, who used to appear in this poor man's Grand Guignol of M. Slepyan's?"

"Ah, there is a sad tale," answered Grandville with a sympathetic wheeze. "After the company failed, LePlaut fell in with evil companions. When last I heard he was working as a dishwasher in a low dive in Montmartre."

"Do you perhaps recall the name of the place?"

"I believe it was called Le Demon des Glaces."

"Well, enough of this pleasant chitcat about days gone

by and vanished friends.'' The Great Lorenzo rubbed his
hands together and turned away from the poster. ''Let me
see the costumes I need.''

Whistling, and not a franc poorer, the magician exited
the costume shop some twenty minutes later. He carried a
large parcel wrapped in green paper under his arm.

He had covered a little more than a half block when a
closed carriage, pulled by a handsome black steed, rolled
up alongside him. When the window shade was raised and
an extremely pretty blonde woman of no more than thirty-
five smiled out at him, the Great Lorenzo nodded and
tipped his bowler hat.

The door opened and the blonde, who wore a dress of
satin and lace and a white fur stole, called out to him in a
sweet voice. ''Is that all you have for such an old and dear
friend as Yvonne Turek? No more than a flick of your hat,
dear Lorenzo?''

The carriage stopped and so did the magician. ''Ah,
forgive me, dear lady, I was woolgathering.''

She pouted attractively. ''Ah, only a few scant years
ago, my dear dumpling, and you could not tear yourself
from my side. My name was on your adorable lips from
noon till night.''

Easing closer to the carriage, he scrutinized its lovely
occupant. ''One can well believe that, for you are a most
attractive creature, Yvonne.''

Extending a gloved hand, she tugged delicately at his
sleeve. ''Why not, for the sake of old times, ride at least a
short way with me?''

''Don't mind if I do.'' Shifting the package, grunting and
huffing, he scrambled into the dark interior.

Reaching around him, Yvonne shut the door. ''Is this
not wonderful?''

The carriage was thick with the scent of jasmine. As
soon as the door had closed, it resumed clacking along the
street.

"It is more than wonderful, dear lady," the magician told her, "since you have never in your entire life met me before."

She sighed and reached into the beaded white purse. "I feared this ruse might not work," she said, producing a pearl-handled .32 revolver and pressing it into his portly side.

Chapter 6

Jennie sat, hands in her lap, gazing out the window of her small hotel room. The midday sky was growing increasingly grey. "My room is quite a bit smaller than yours," she mentioned. "Must be difficult for you, since you're in the mood to pace."

"I don't enjoy posh hotels and ritzy suites. That's my father's idea, says it keeps up the image and reputation of the Challenge International Detective Agency." Skirting her brass bed, Harry paced along the edge of the Persian rug. "Wish I had Lorenzo's gift of second sight, then I'd know where the hell he is." He tugged out his pocket watch again.

"He really does have some sort of unusual power," said the reporter. "I've exposed a lot of bunco artists and fake mediums, but he's authentic. Coming to the museum the way he did last night, simply getting off his train and rushing to Paris."

"Sure, he's got a gift." Harry frowned at his watch before returning it to his pocket. "He's also fairly shrewd. Sometimes he can con you into thinking a lucky guess is a mystical message from beyond."

The sky continued to darken; a wind rattled the windows.

Jennie said, "This plan you've worked out for getting inside Max Orchardson's lair is—"

"We've worked out," he corrected. "You were in on the—"

"As a bystander mostly. You and Lorenzo outvoted me every time I attempted to express a little reasonable doubt as—"

"That's the essence of democracy. The will of the majority is—"

"Well, this representative of the minority is going to be just as dead as you two hooligans should this crack-brained—"

"Audacious. Our scheme is audacious, not crack-brained."

Standing, she faced him. "I don't want any of us to get hurt. No newspaper story is that important, no detective investigation either."

"This is a different Jennie Barr," he said, grinning. "You were claiming only yesterday that getting the story for the New York *Daily Inquirer* was more important than—"

"Could you let up a bit, Harry. I wasn't exactly myself yesterday and I'm feeling low enough without your—"

"Okay, sorry." He crossed to her and put his hands on her shoulders. "We'll all come out of this all right."

"You're concerned about Lorenzo already, though, aren't you? Because he's late."

"He's only . . ." Harry let go of her to pull out his watch. "Damn, nearly a half hour late."

"Keep in mind he's a very romantic soul. This is spring and we're in Paris."

"I suppose he might've made a stop to see that lady with the cork leg." He glanced at the door. "He usually doesn't dally when he's helping out on something like this, though."

"Where was he going to pick up the costumes and all?"

"Shop of an old friend of his."

"You know where it is?"

"Just off the Avenue Montaigne," Harry answered. "We'll give him maybe another half hour, then go over there to . . ." He put his finger to his lips, hunched slightly and ran over to yank the room door open.

The dark brown corridor was empty, but a pale blue envelope lay on the flowered carpeting.

Bending, Harry picked it up. "Addressed to me in Lorenzo's handwriting." After shutting the door, he opened the message. " 'My dear colleagues, There have been several new and illuminating developments. Thus a small change of plans is called for. Meet me by no later than two at the address below. And, Harry my boy, be absolutely *certain* you aren't followed. Ever yours, the Great Lorenzo.' "

Jennie frowned. "This could be a trap."

"It could," he agreed. "But we'll have to go over there to make sure."

Looping his arm around the stone chimney, Harry used his free hand to pull Jennie up the slanting slate roof.

The rain, light thus far, had begun to fall just as they'd leaped over to this rooftop from the three story pension next door.

Slowly and carefully Jennie worked her way up through the maze of chimney pots and stovepipes to Harry's side. She was wearing her Norfolk suit and cap. "The balcony of number 104 Rue Brindavoine ought to be directly below the apex of this darn roof."

"Yep, so I'll lower you down and then join you."

"Be careful on this slate; rain's making it slippery."

"I've had quite a lot of experience climbing roofs." He took hold of her arm and pulled her down into a crouch with him. "By the way, how do you go about buying a man's suit?"

"I got this in the Boy's Department of Estling's Universal Emporium in London last year." She kept close to him as he progressed toward the front edge of the apartment building roof. "Told them it was actually for my nephew Harry, an unattractive and rather dim lad whom I was nonetheless attached to."

"You didn't try it on then?"

"No, but it fits just fine. You really are very provincial, Harry."

"Little baggy in the seat."

"No, it isn't. I'm certain of that because only last evening I was pinched on the Rue—"

"Hush for now." He was flat out on the tilting roof, the afternoon rain pelting lightly down on him.

Harry tugged himself until he was out over the edge and could get a glimpse of the wrought iron balcony below.

There was someone standing on it now, under the shelter of a pink parasol.

The parasol started to spin and after a half dozen turns was lowered to one side.

The Great Lorenzo was beaming up at him. "I'm greatly impressed by your acrobatic entrance, my boy," he said. "Yet since time is important, it would have been better to have availed yourselves of the doorway downstairs."

The Great Lorenzo was using the rolled up parasol as a pointer. Aiming it at the blonde woman who sat stiffly in the cane-bottom chair, he announced, "This charming damsel is Yvonne Turek—or rather that's the name she assumed for her part in this intrigue. In reality she is Yvette Tardi, a gifted yet, sadly, unemployed actress."

"And who's the gent dozing on the floor yonder?" asked Harry.

"He is Manuel Bulcão, an import from Lisbon," said the magician as he pointed the ferrule of the parasol at him. "He's not in a hypnotic trance, as is the fair Yvonne. Him I conked on the noggin and trussed up, using some of the impressive knots I learned during a recent cruise of the Mediterranean."

"Who are those folks exactly?" Jennie was standing near the crackling fire in the small marble fireplace. "Do they work for Max Orchardson?"

"On the contrary," the Great Lorenzo said. "They are in the employ of the opposition.

Harry settled into an armchair next to a marble-top table. He drummed his fingertips on the base of the hurricane lamp for a few seconds. "Opposed to us or to Orchardson?"

"Both." He took a few steps away from the entranced blonde, shoes clicking on the black and white mosaic tiles of the parlor floor. "You have both no doubt heard of a gentleman named Anwar Zaytoon."

"The Merchant of Death," said Harry.

"Just about the most powerful arms dealer in the world," added Jennie as she held her cap to the fireplace. "I tried to interview him once in Constantinople and three of his toadies came darn close to tossing me in a public fountain. A very mysterious, not at all cordial man."

Harry asked, "Is Zaytoon interested in the obelisk?"

"Very much so." The Great Lorenzo nodded at the blonde actress. "She was hired to entice me here and make me an offer of ten thousand francs to double-cross you and become an informant for Zaytoon."

"You're worth more than that."

"Twice at least," agreed the magician. "Apparently our death merchant is aware you're in Paris, Harry. He's had your hotel watched and your movements scrutinized. Which is how they became aware of my advent upon the scene and why I warned you to shake off any tails before venturing here to share in the fair Yvonne's reluctant hospitality."

"Why," asked Jennie, "is everyone so interested in the Osiris Obelisk?"

"Yvonne is—forgive me for stating this so bluntly, dear lady—only an underling who knows little of the motives of the sinister Mr. Zaytoon."

"He's in Paris now?"

"Nearby."

Getting up, Harry went to the window they'd recently

climbed in through and looked down at the rain-swept street. A mournful black carriage was rolling by. "What about the mummy—who was he working for?"

"Zaytoon. I determined, only moments before Yvonne put her ill-fated plan to lure me into a life of espionage and trickery into effect, that he was a seedy actor named LePlaut. The lady confirmed that."

"They wanted to scare off all the guards," said Harry, "and then steal the obelisk?"

"That's it exactly."

Jennie said, "It's sort of ugly and squatty, not worth anywhere near as much as some of the other artifacts at the museum."

"Ah, my child, but it apparently holds some secret," the magician told her. "A secret worth killing for, a secret even worth trying to corrupt a man of my sterling character for."

Chapter 7

Every few feet a thin tree grew up from a small plot of ground surrounded by sidewalk. The narrow trunk of each was guarded by a circular fence of wrought iron. The rain hit hard at the trees and made them shiver.

The carriage, borrowed from the unprotesting Yvonne, had been left around the corner, the dark horse tethered to one of the frail trees.

Held high above the heads of the three of them was an immense black umbrella the Great Lorenzo had found in a compartment under the driver's seat of the carriage he'd driven here to the suburb of Neuilly-sur-Seine.

"Don't fret should you get splashed by the elements, my boy," the magician told Harry, shifting his grip on the ebony umbrella handle. "The makeup I've expertly applied to our visages is one hundred percent waterproof."

"I wasn't worrying about that." Harry reached up to adjust the crimson fez he was wearing. "Instead, I was wondering if Orchardson will fall for this."

The Great Lorenzo brushed at the striped kaftan he was wearing. "You forget he is extremely eager to obtain the obelisk," he reminded. "He covets the thing, despite its cursed nature. He will be, therefore, anxious to believe the yarn we're going to spin. We are two high-placed Egyptian officials, extremely close to his Highness the Khedive. On our handsome persons we carry authentic documents proving beyond a shadow of a doubt that the obelisk in question doesn't rightly belong to the Musée des Antiquités at all. Orchardson will dote on us, never fear, and be elated at what looks like a chance to purchase the object he seeks."

They'd reached an iron-barred gate in a high wall of pale brownish stone.

Jennie swallowed hard. "This is it, Max Orchardson's villa," she said. "I'm supposed to yank this bellpull three times."

"Go ahead and do it," said Harry.

"I don't think I like you with a beard."

"Neither do I. Ring."

"Once we're inside," said the Great Lorenzo, "I'll use my superior hypnotic powers on the fellow and we'll find out all we want to know. Ring, child."

Shrugging, Jennie tugged the dangling black chain.

Through the gates they could see a half acre of grounds covered with hedges long untrimmed, high grass and tall shaggy pines. Beyond that loomed a sprawling stone house, turreted, that was the exact shade of the rainy afternoon.

Before the third tug of the bellpull a dog was barking, a deep gruff bark that seemed to be coming from a large hollow room.

"Let's hope," said Harry, "we can convince the dog we're Egyptian officials."

"Hounds are no problem," the magician assured him. "In my vanished youth I toured the States in the company of, among others, Professor Swaim and his Educated Canines. He imparted to me the tricks of the . . . Ah, this must be the butler."

A huge black man in a frock coat and striped trousers was walking methodically down a grey gravel path toward them. He carried no umbrella and appeared to be oblivious of the rain.

Halting a few yards from the locked gate, he gave Jennie an inquiring stare. "What is the meaning of this, missy?"

"I was told to come here," she answered. "Today. At three."

"Alone," the butler said.

"Well, I intended to be, but these gentlemen approached me at the museum last evening and insisted on tagging along. They claim to have a proposition."

"It is?"

"We are in a position to sell your employer the Osiris Obelisk," said the Great Lorenzo. "Assuming that he, whoever he may be, is interested."

"Who," asked the black man in his deep rumbling voice, "might you be, sir?"

Tugging impatiently at his beard, the magician said, "Ah, but of course, my fame does not extend to foreign climes such as this. I am, my good man, Mohammed Ali Pasha." He bowed. "My young associate is Cherif Pasha. We both represent the Khedive of Egypt and come equipped with papers proving the obelisk in question is rightfully ours."

"It is," added Harry, "our wish to sell it to the highest bidder."

Stepping forward, the butler unlocked the heavy gate. "Please to enter."

"To hear is to obey." The Great Lorenzo bowed once more before stepping through the open gateway.

The black man waited until all three of them were on the villa grounds and then relocked the gate. From beneath his frock coat he brought forth a .45 revolver. "If you'll step inside the house, Mr. Challenge, Mr. Lorenzo and Miss Barr," he suggested, "I'm certain Mr. Orchardson will be quite pleased to see you all."

The living room was on the top floor of the villa. Vast, high-ceilinged, with peach-colored walls. There was little furniture and all of it was huddled in the room's center around a white potbellied stove. Except for a worn Oriental carpet on which rested a divan, two mauve armchairs, a claw-footed table and a bust of Voltaire, the hardwood floors were bare.

"Come in, come in, you three," invited Max Orchardson. "Like most recluses I simply can't stand to be alone."

He was lounging on the maroon divan, a three-hundred-pound man who seemed to be made of partially risen bread dough. His face was puffy and dead white, his close-cropped hair the color of driven snow. An enormous silken smoking jacket was wrapped around him, a pattern of exploding orchids decorating the taut silk.

"You've lost a bit of weight, Orchardson." Harry scratched at his thick false beard. "Judging from the last society page portrait of you I saw."

"Yes, I do believe I'm wasting away from worry," he said. "Those of us who loathe life as much as I do have a terrible fear of death. It might turn out to be even more boring."

The black butler cleared his throat with a sedate rumble. "Shall I fetch the hot coals and the pokers, sir?"

"Not yet, Logo." The languid fat man stretched and plucked a green carnation from the lacquered vase on the table. "Suppose, Challenge, you tell me what you have in mind with this delightful masquerade."

Harry moved across the hardwood floor to the edge of the rug. "We're all interested in the obelisk. We wanted to find out how much you knew about it."

"There was no need to dress up like a pair of road-show Othellos to do that, dear boy," Orchardson pointed out, brushing at his puffy cheek with the green flower. "No, you intended to take me unawares."

"I'm not too happy over what you did to Jennie." Harry scratched at his false whiskers once again. "These damn things are starting to itch."

"The price of duplicity." Orchardson pushed himself to a sitting position and the divan gave a protesting moan. "If I catch your drift, Challenge, you had in mind to find out all that I was up to and perhaps give me a sound thrashing as well.''

"I still may."

Orchardson blinked. Then he started laughing, a whooping, gasping noise. "Forgive me," he apologized after a moment, "I fear my grief expresses itself in odd ways. I even laughed at my mother's funeral."

"He's grieving for you," explained the large Logo, "because you'll soon be dead."

After giving his fez an adjusting shove, the Great Lorenzo went striding over to the center of the room. "What say we get down to business," he said. "You don't want to kill us because then you won't have a chance at the obelisk. Nor will you be able to find out what sort of a deal we're contemplating with your chief rival."

Orchardson's colorless eyebrows climbed. "Who might that be?"

"Let us refer to him merely as the Merchant of Death."

"A colorful name." Orchardson poked the stem of the emerald-dyed carnation into his doughy chin as he glanced toward the wide windows at the front of the room. The rain was pelting the thick panes. "Not one that means anything to me."

"He's certainly aware of you. In fact, this very day he offered us, via an emissary, a considerable sum to arrange for the delivery of the obelisk into his hands." The Great Lorenzo pushed his fez to a more jaunty angle. "We'll, of course, entertain a higher offer."

Orchardson waved the green carnation at Logo. "You'd best start bringing in the torture implements," he said. "This polite social intercourse has started to be quite tedious." His pale lips seemed to disappear into his flesh as he smiled. "We'll begin with the lady, since I have never gone along with the rather antiquated dictum that young people should be seen and not heard."

"The iron boot, sir?"

"To start." Orchardson plucked a few petals from the

flower and suffered another fit of laughter. Two flaring pink spots of color decorated his pudgy cheeks as he rocked back and forth on the creaking divan. "Ah, I do wish I could express my deep sorrow for Miss Barr in a more seemly fashion." He flung the smashed petals to the rug.

"You do anything to her," warned Harry, "and you'll never get the secret of eternal life."

Orchardson suddenly stiffened, his three hundred pounds freezing. Finally he asked, "Whatever are you talking about, dear boy?"

Grinning, Harry nodded at the Great Lorenzo and then started scratching at his beard. "Now," he said.

The portly magician threw himself to the left, snatching off his fez as he headed for the floor. Concealed in the hat was a pearl-handled .32 revolver. He shot Logo twice in his gun arm before the black man could swing his own weapon around to fire.

Jennie, meantime, had dropped flat out on the hardwood.

And Harry had yanked out the derringer that had been taped under his bushy Egyptian beard.

He pointed the gun at the seated Orchardson.

The fat man did a sudden and unexpected thing. He executed a perfect, graceful backward somersault off the divan. Landing on his slippered feet, Orchardson ran surprisingly rapidly toward the high, wide windows. Not even pausing to open one, he went crashing through it and out.

"Holy Christ!" Harry sprinted to the shattered window.

He was about to look down for a glimpse of the fat man's broken body on the grounds far below, when two shots came whistling in at him from out in the rainy afternoon.

Harry hit the floor, rolled out of range.

Looking out, he saw another of the giant bats flying away through the rain-swept sky. Clutched in its talons was a laughing Orchardson.

*　　*　　*

The black butler was sitting on the floor. "Forgive me, gentlemen and lady." He slapped his good hand to his mouth, swallowed. "You shan't have the opportunity to question me." His eyes snapped shut and he fell over backwards on the bare floor.

Harry lunged, tried to pry the man's mouth open. "Damn it."

"Is he dead?" asked Jennie.

"Nope, looks like some kind of trance."

Squatting, the Great Lorenzo sniffed at the comatose butler. "It's maracuya, an obscure herbal drug used by certain mean-minded tribes of the upper Amazon," he concluded. "Friend Logo will be dead to the world for weeks to come."

Jennie had wandered over near the divan. "Here's something." She lifted up the vase of green carnations. "A little wooden panel full of buttons. That must be how Orchardson summoned that bat and had it hovering outside the window."

"Bats are notoriously difficult to train, child." The magician huffed to an upright position. "I seriously doubt one could be induced to come running every time a buzzer sounded."

"This isn't a regular everyday bat." Harry joined Jennie to examine the control panel. "Fact is, Lorenzo, it's probably a flying mechanism of some sort."

"Impossible. Successful flight is years off, its secret yet to be revealed to mortal man."

Jennie perched on the divan edge. "Speaking of secrets, Harry, why did you taunt Orchardson by saying you were on to the secret of eternal life?"

He grinned. "That's got to be what's behind all this interest in the obelisk," he told her. "Remember that odd inscription Allegre translated for us? Orchardson is ailing and Zaytoon, from what I've heard, is up near ninety. Both of them are especially interested in immortality and they must have the notion that somehow the obelisk can give that to them.''

''Though still in my prime and in tip-top shape, I must admit that I, too, have entertained the idea of living beyond my allotted time,'' admitted the Great Lorenzo. ''Not for selfish reasons, mind you, but because of my exceptional gifts. It seems unfair to keep generations as yet unborn from enjoying an evening of my magical entertainments. My fabled Floating Lady illusion, for instance, belongs to the ages. Even the Japanese Diving—''

''Hey.'' Harry tugged out a small drawer that had been concealed beneath the marble top of the small table. ''Some letters and a few pages torn out of a magazine.''

''Those pages are from *The Journal of Advanced Technology*, published in England,'' recognized Jennie.

''Dated April 1892. Article's entitled '*The "Flying Machine" of Professor G. P. R. Stowe Successfully Tested.*' Goes on to describe the flights of a steam-powered craft Stowe calls an aerodrome.''

''Oh, I interviewed him three or four years ago when he was in New York trying to raise funds.'' Jennie shook her head and wrinkled her freckled nose. ''He struck me as an eccentric and probably a charlatan.''

''This aerodrome, though, would look quite a bit like a giant bat with a few modifications,'' said Harry.

Taking the tearsheets from him, she studied the steel-engraved drawings. ''Maybe you're right at that. Orchardson might have Professor Stowe working for him.''

''One way or the other.''

''Ah, listen to this.'' The magician was thumbing through the letters. ''These missives are from various physicians in Great Britain and the continent. The general medical opinion is that unless Orchardson suspends his decadent style of living only a miracle can keep him alive more than a few months.''

''A good motive for going after immortality,'' said Harry. ''I'm wondering, though, why everybody waited until now to make a try for the obelisk. It's been sitting in the damn museum for months.''

''Let's search the villa,'' said Jennie. ''The answer may be here someplace.''

For the rest of the rainy afternoon, until twilight took over, they went through the rented villa. But they found nothing more of interest.

Chapter 8

The horse-drawn omnibus made an unscheduled stop directly in front of the Musée des Antiquités. On the open upper level the Great Lorenzo stood up, adjusted his Inverness cape and started for the metal stairway. To the scattering of perplexed open-air passengers he said, "I hope, dear friends, you'll be able to avail yourselves of the free passes to the Great Lorenzo's magical extravaganza. I hear he's tops and well worth a twenty-six-hour journey to nearby Urbania."

He paused by a pretty nursemaid who had a chubby little boy in a sailor suit in her care. "And for the little admiral . . ." From the mid-morning air he plucked a bottle containing a model of a full-rigged clipper ship.

"Where's the crew?" inquired the sour-faced little fellow as he accepted the gift with sticky hands.

"For you, dear lady . . ." A bouquet of yellow roses appeared in his gloved hand. Bowing, he presented them to her.

"Oh, monsieur. I am quite . . . taken aback."

"And well you should be, dear Albertine. Adieu for now."

"Oh, but how did you know my name?"

He tipped his bowler, which was the color of green tree moss. "It is my business to know things." Bowing again, he then went hurrying and clanging down the stairs.

The uniformed conductor helped him to the sidewalk and handed him his plump portmanteau. "A pleasure to have served such an important official, Inspector Swann."

"Your duty to France will not go unrewarded, Gallimard." The Great Lorenzo saluted him briskly and then grabbed up his suitcase.

The pair of sturdy horses began moving again and the omnibus with its nonplussed passengers rolled away down the street.

Ascending the museum steps two at a time, the Great Lorenzo tried the brass doorknob.

The heavy door was locked.

He started knocking on it enthusiastically with his fist. "I have a train to catch."

After a moment the door was opened a fraction and a lean, moustached man who was obviously a plainclothes police detective peered out. "The museum is not open to the public at this time, monsieur."

"I know that, which is why I've been standing out here for untold minutes rapping on the door." The Great Lorenzo thrust a well-shod foot into the opening. "Were you as perceptive as one in your profession ought well to be, my friend, you would have noticed that I am far from being a member of the public. Nay, I happen to be a confidential operative for the prestigious Challenge International Detective Agency."

"Ah, yes. M. Challenge, accompanied by a very charming young lady, is within this institution at this very moment."

"That fact, my colleague, accounts for my being upon your doorstep."

"Come in then, M. . . . I fear I don't know your name."

"I am the Great Lorenzo."

"Indeed? An unusual name for a private investigator, is it not?"

The magician pushed his way into the museum. "I

happen to be an unorthodox sleuth.'' He went striding along the corridor toward the director's private office.

"Yes, your very attire gave me a clue to that fact." The policeman remained at the entrance.

Knocking twice, the Great Lorenzo let himself in to Maurice Allegre's office. "Excuse my intrusion, one and all," he said, taking off his hat and dropping it on the edge of a large alabaster casket. "I also request there be no tears and handwringing when I make my sad announcement."

Allegre had hopped to his feet. "Who in the world is this uncouth—"

"One of my operatives." Harry rose from his chair. "What's happening, Lorenzo?"

"You sound very dire," observed Jennie from the other chair in front of the desk.

"I must, alas, take the very next train to Urbania's fun-filled capital of Kaltzonburg," he announced ruefully. "It seems the madcap heir to the throne, Prince Rudolph, has insisted on a special command performance of my entire magical evening. The manager of the Spielzeug Theater wired me at the crack of dawn. Therefore, I needs must cut short my stay in this magnificient city and rush across field and fen to Urbania. Prince Rudy is not a fellow one offends or disappoints, especially when one intends to play three, possibly four, weeks in his domain."

"As it turns out," Harry told him, "I'll be leaving Paris for Urbania in a couple of days myself."

"We'll be leaving," modified Jennie.

"Oh, so? That's splendid news and goes far toward explaining the vision I was visited with as the new day's rosy fingers touched at my eyelids," said the Great Lorenzo. "For I saw the three of us—you were excluded, M. Allegre—Yes, I saw you and I, Harry my boy, along with you, dear Jennie, together in Urbania and languishing in . . . Ah, but the setting is of no import."

"What was it?"

"Well, a dungeon. But you know these images, these

portents of the future, are rarely one hundred percent accurate.'' After smiling at them all, he put his hat back on. "Until we meet again, dear friends.''

"Bon voyage.'' Jennie got to her feet and kissed him on the cheek.

"By the way, Harry," he said as they shook hands, "my hotel is still being watched by somebody's toadies. I had to duck down several quaint Paris byways and then commandeer an omnibus to throw them off the scent. Farewell for now, no tears.'' He gathered up his heavy portmanteau and took his leave.

Allegre sank back into his desk chair. "An omnibus?"

"Merely a figure of speech,'' Harry assured him. "Let's get back to business.''

"There is but little more to discuss, M. Challenge,'' he said. "As I was explaining before your corpulent associate burst in, Baron Felix Groll has decided, because of certain unfortunate incidents here at the museum, that he wants the Osiris Obelisk shipped to him even earlier than planned. It will be crated and ready to travel, by way of a special train, two days hence. You, as well as two of Inspector Swann's best men, shall travel with it. And, let me add, I wish you luck.''

The restaurant floated leisurely along the darkening Seine. Its upper deck was ringed with softly glowing paper lanterns. At the cluster of small tables sat gentlemen in dark suits and top hats, women in stylish frocks and hats. On the small platform at the stern of the riverboat was a trio of hefty young men in straw hats and tight, striped blazers. They were playing exuberantly romantic music on concertina, guitar and violin.

The lights along the banks of the river were coming on, reflected yellow and gold in the water.

Harry had an elbow resting on their small checkered tablecloth. "You've fallen silent,'' he mentioned.

Jennie stroked the stem of her wineglass idly. "I dislike

using trite phrases," she said, "and so I've been sitting here trying to come up with a fresh, brand-new way of saying how wonderful this all is."

He grinned. "We're both off duty."

"Very well, then it's a wonderful evening and I'm very fond of you," she told him. "The dinner was lovely and I wish we didn't have to leave Paris for Urbania day after tomorrow."

"We'd have to, even if I didn't have to guard the obelisk and you didn't have to write about it," he said. "Lorenzo gave us a pair of free passes to his show."

"As much as I admire his showmanship, I doubt I'd travel hundreds of miles by rail to see him. Although he is . . . What's the matter, Harry?"

"Nothing."

She started to turn to look in the direction he'd been looking. "You saw something that—"

"Keep your eyes on me." He put his hand over hers.

"What is it I'm not staring at?"

"Couple husky fellows wearing Zouave uniforms and sitting at a table near the opposite railing."

"I hadn't noticed them."

"Only came up from the saloon below about ten minutes ago."

"Why are they causing you to scowl?"

"For one thing they've been, very unobtrusively they think, keeping an eye on us since they got up here," he said. "For another, their uniforms aren't quite authentic. Costume shop stuff."

"There's certainly been a lot of dressing up going on lately."

"I didn't spot these boys following us earlier, so maybe they're only interested in pretty red-haired lady reporters."

"Auburn," she corrected. "My hair isn't red."

"Should they make a move, just duck under our table and let me—"

"Like heck I will. I've been a newspaper reporter for

eight years. A couple of louts in fezes and pantaloons don't scare—''

''Relax, they may not have anything to do with the obelisk.''

''Seems like just about everybody in Paris does,'' she said. ''Max Orchardson, Anwar Zaytoon and lord knows who else. Do you think that hunk of granite really does contain the secret of eternal life?''

''Doesn't matter what I think,'' answered Harry. ''Orchardson and Zaytoon are obviously convinced—and I'd like to know who or what convinced them all this time after the thing was hauled here from Egypt.''

''I've been looking into that angle.'' She reached into her purse for her notebook. ''After we parted company this afternoon I called on a few people I know in Paris.''

''You were supposed to stay in your room.''

''C'mon, it's unlikely Orchardson'll try to hypnotize me twice. And most other threats I can cope with.''

Harry shrugged. ''Who'd you talk to and what'd you find out?''

''About four months ago, and this initial information I got from Allegre himself, a onetime professor from the University of Graustark spent a week at the Musée des Antiquités,'' she said as she opened her notebook. ''He devoted a good deal of his time to photographing and measuring the Osiris Obelisk. He got, according to Allegre, quite excited on his last day there. Left abruptly at midday, never to return. His name is Alexander Fodorsky.''

''You talked to some of your contacts about Fodorsky?''

''I did, and it turns out his reputation of late has been sort of unsavory,'' the auburn-haired reporter replied. ''He'd been a reputable scholar up until two years ago, which is why Allegre let him hang around. His special fields are Egyptology and Orientology. More recently, however, he's grown interested in sorcery and the black arts.''

''Any links between him and Orchardson?''

"Fodorsky is rumored to have been a house guest of his in London last winter."

Harry leaned back, glancing up at the deepening night overhead. "Fodorsky must've found out something about the obelisk, something Courdard and his colleagues may not've been aware of. He passed the news on to Orchardson."

"And somehow Zaytoon got wind of the secret, too."

Harry said, "Why is Orchardson killing off everybody who was on the expedition?"

"He can't be certain they don't know something about the secret. So he eliminates them." She shut her notebook. "In a way I'm disappointed there really isn't a curse. With a good ancient curse my paper's guaranteed syndication of my articles all over the—"

"Our Zouaves," cut in Harry, "are making a move."

Casually she looked over. "They do seem to be, don't they?"

The two husky men, decked out in fezes, short blue jackets loaded with glittering medals, baggy red trousers and white leggings, were coming toward them as rapidly as they could across the crowded restaurant deck. Each was holding a wicked-looking dagger in his teeth.

"Sure you don't want to hide under the—"

"Hooey."

The larger Zouave arrived first. "I am insulted," he snarled around the knife handle. "I can stand no more. You, monsieur, have been making snide faces and wicked gestures at myself and my companion for far too long."

"The honor of the regiment is at stake." His broad-shouldered companion took his knife from his teeth to his hand.

"Fellows," said Harry, grinning amiably up at them, "I suggest you forget about the honor of your alleged regiment and go quietly back to your table before you find yourselves picking your backsides up off the deck."

"Gar! He insults us further." The bigger of the two grabbed his knife from between his jagged teeth.

"I'll take this one," Harry said across the table.

He unexpectedly brought up his foot and kicked the Zouave resoundingly in the groin.

The tassle of the man's fez stood up straight. He yowled, doubled up and clutched at himself.

Harry kicked him in the knee. He then stood, grabbed the belligerent Zouave by his thick neck and, seemingly with little effort, tossed him clean over the railing.

A paper lantern got tangled with the Zouave and it fell, shedding sparks, down to the dark Seine with him.

Jennie had worked less flamboyantly. She'd punched her surprised Zouave hard in the midsection, whacked him across the shin with a spare chair. Before he fully recovered from that, Jennie shoved him against the railing, booted him in the backside and then tipped him over into the river below.

"Very deft," said Harry just after the second splash.

Smiling, she rested her elbows on the railing and watched their two bedraggled attackers go swimming toward a stone quay. "I suppose, Harry, we really should've kept at least one of those louts to ask questions of and all."

"Maybe," he admitted. "Thing is, whenever I get into a brawl alongside a body of water, the temptation to toss everybody in is too much."

Smiling, she straightened up the things atop their table and seated herself again. "Do you want to explain this incident to the waiter who's running over here now? Or shall I?"

"I'll handle it," he offered. "Least I can do."

Chapter 9

On the morning the obelisk was to leave Paris Harry awoke an hour ahead of daybreak.

He hopped free of his brass bed, grabbed his Colt .38 from the bedside table and sprinted to the door.

Yanking it open, he got ready to dodge.

"I say, those are rather smashing underdrawers, Mr. Challenge. Jove, you Americans do have a flair for that sort of—"

"Who the hell are you?"

The young man was wearing a tweedy traveling suit and a deerstalker cap. His face was long, lean and deeply tanned and there was a monocle shielding his left eye. "One is rather impressed, don't you know, by the acuity of your hearing," he said. "I mean to say, I was approaching on tiptoe so as not to awaken any of your fellow guests in this jolly hotel and yet—"

"Who," repeated Harry, pointing the revolver at his visitor's breastbone, "are you?"

"Ah, deuced rude of me, old man." He smiled a toothy smile. "Name is Albert Melville Pennoyer. Just about everyone, from the mater on down, calls me Bertie. Rather a chummy sort of name I— "

"Why are you pussyfooting outside my door at this ungodly hour?"

"Is beastly early, ain't it?" Pennoyer shrugged his narrow shoulders. "Yet if one wants to catch a ride on this deuced secret train, one had best be up and doing with the proverbial cock, eh?"

Taking a step back, Harry asked, "What secret train?"

"What? Oh, I see, yes." He put his gloved right hand over his mouth before chuckling. "Very clever of you, old bean, pretending to know nothing of the Osiris Obelisk. Admirable example of the sort of cunning and duplicity one expects from the Challenge International Detective Agency."

Frowning, Harry said, "Bertie Pennoyer. Wait now, you're one of the five who led the expedition."

"Very good. Mind like a steel trap. Good show. Spotted me right off." He hid another appreciative chuckle. "When I inform you I've fair got the wind up, Challenge old chap, you'll understand why."

"You figure you may go the way of Reynard Courdaud and Sir Munson Bellhouse."

"Rightho, not to mention Emil Koontzman."

"Did something happen to him?"

"Just yesterday in the Bavarian Alps . . . I say, might I come inside, old man. Confessing cowardice in a public hallway is deuced awkward."

"Sure, come on." Harry stood aside. "What's that stuck to your shoe?"

"Rather imagine it's a cablegram from your dear pater." Bending from the waist, Pennoyer detached the flimsy envelope from the sole of his shoe and passed it to Harry. "Saw the thing, don't you know, when I was girding up the proverbial loins to knock upon your portal. Stepped in some muck while sightseeing in Montmartre last evening, you know. Thought I'd succeeded in scraping it all off. Sorry."

"How'd you know my father'd be cabling me?" After elbowing the door shut, he tore the envelope open.

"Well, old man, I rather hoped he would. Since we

exchanged wires yesterday. Soon as I heard of poor Emil's fate.''

The message from Harry's father said:

> *Dear Son: A brainless ninny named Bertie Pennoyer wants a bodyguard to see him safely to Urbania. Loaded with dough. Bundle him up on that special train you told me about. Your loving father, the Challenge International Detective Agency.*

Refolding the message, Harry tossed it on his rumpled bed. ''What happened to Dr. Koontzman?''

''According to preliminary reports, the poor blighter was attacked by vampire bats while mountaineering,'' answered the nervous young man. ''Odd place for such creatures, one would think. Much too cold.''

''How did you find out about the train?''

Pennoyer let his monocle pop free and caught it in his palm. ''Simple, old thing. Visited Maurice Allegre yesterday and he— ''

''That nitwit wasn't supposed to tell anyone about—''

''But, I say, Challenge. I am not just anyone, eh?'' He began polishing the lens on his silk pocket handkerchief. ''I mean to say, I'm a highly esteemed amateur archaeologist. I did, afterall, finance the whole bloody, you'll forgive my coarse lingo, expedition to the Valley of Jackals. Continually doing that sort of thing, don't you know. Entire Pennoyer clan filthy rich. Great grandfather made a pile out in India. By exploiting the wogs and the fuzzy-wuzzies, so family tradition has it.''

''Has there been an attempt on your life?''

''Not that one is aware of, no. Haven't noticed huge vampire bats flapping about one's digs and all that.''

Setting his gun back on the table, Harry started getting dressed. ''As of now there's only you and—''

''I say, shall I turn my back, old chap? Some blokes crave a bit of privacy while—''

"Up to you." Harry tugged his trousers on. "Only you and Lady Jane Bedlumm are still alive, of the five who headed up the expedition."

Pennoyer shuddered. "All this beastly talk of death makes one deuced aware of one's mortality, don't you know," he said. "Lady Jane's a formidable old girl. In Tibet somewhere at last report. Seeking spiritual enlightment from some silly sounding bloke called the Ringding Gelong Lama. Doubt the rascals'll find the old girl there."

"Any notion who wants you dead?"

"Not the foggiest."

"Or why?"

"Supposed to be a curse on the obelisk. Never believed that rot before. But now."

Harry buttoned his shirt. "Know Max Orchardson?"

"By reputation. Believe he was asked to leave one of my London clubs a few years ago. Never met the fellow. Wouldn't want to. Why do you ask?"

"He's interested in the obelisk."

"Suppose he would be. Goes in for a lot of magical nonsense. Not a gentleman, you know."

Sitting on the edge of his bed, Harry pulled on a sock. "What about Anwar Zaytoon?"

"The Merchant of Death chap?" He masked a small chuckle. "Never met the bloke personally, but did see a rather amusing cartoon of him in one of the weeklies not long ago. Artist—clever chaps these artists, how they do it beats me—this artist, I say, depicted old Zaytoon as a vulture, don't you know, feeding on a fat corpse that was labeled Ungodly Munitions Profits. Awfully droll. Has the old boy been paying attention to the obelisk also?"

"Some, yes."

"Can't, for the life of me, figure out why." He fitted his polished monocle back into his eye. "Not much of an obelisk as obelisks go. I mean to say, the blooming one they've got right here in Paris beats it all hollow. Midget by comparison. Truth to tell, Challenge old man, I'd just as soon we'd left the thing there in the sand. Others insisted." He shook his head. "Understand Baron Groll paid a pretty penny for it and, which I ought to be grateful for, he's invited me to spend a few weeks at his estate in Urbania. Wants to jaw about the obelisk, Egypt and all that sort of thing."

"Which is why you want to tag along on this jaunt?"

"Once again, old thing, you've hit the nail on the proverbial head," said young Pennoyer admiringly. "Safe as houses, traveling with you and a trainload of French bobbies. That's how I see it."

"I suppose so, but—"

"Already chatted with Inspector Swann. Last evening. Have a jolly nice note from him giving me the old boy's blessing. Where'd I put the blasted thing?" He began searching his pockets. "Jove, here's that one hundred pounds. Your pater suggested I offer you this as a bonus should you show any reluctance to undertake the job. Are you?"

Harry took the money from his hand. "Not yet, but I might at any moment."

An hour after the special train pulled out of Paris the rain began. A heavy rain, hitting hard at the windows of Harry's compartment.

"Cozy," observed Jennie. She was seated opposite him, next to a basket full of food and wine she'd packed for the journey.

He was watching the new rain fall on the French countryside. "Hum?"

"I was remarking about how cozy I felt," the pretty reporter said. "Our own little five car train. You and I together in a comfortable carriage. Two plainclothes and ten uniformed police along as chaperones. The obelisk all crated up and resting in a burglarproof baggage car. Cozy."

"About that obelisk, Jennie . . ."

"Don't tell me you're starting to believe it's really got a

curse on it. That silly ass Bertie Pennoyer seems to . . . something you want to tell me, Harry?''

He hesitated, then shook his head. "Nope, not really," he said finally. "Well, I am a mite dubious about Bertie Pennoyer and that's what I've been sitting here thinking about. Seems hard to believe anybody can actually be as dim-witted and fatuous as he pretends to be.''

Jennie laughed. "There are numbers of the very best people in Merry England who'd refute you, Harry," she said. "Bertie Pennoyer is simply not very bright. He is, because of the impressive Pennoyer wealth, very popular in British society. Nobody, though, has ever accused him of having much in the way of brains.''

Harry took out a cigar, glanced at Jennie and put it away again. "So far on this damn case I've encountered quite a few people who have pretended to be what they weren't," he said. "From that guy LePlaut who was trying to pose as a mummy to those imitation Zouaves the other night.''

"You include me on the list? Heartless reporter pretending to love you so she can get her story.''

He grinned. "You're still on the list, but your name's only in pencil.''

"We're always going to have a complicated time of it.'' She rested her hands on her knees. "Because just about every time I run into you I'm interested in the same case you are. That was true of the Blackwood Castle affair and the Electric Man business in London last year and—''

There was a knock on the door.

Harry said, "What?''

The door opened and a bent old man in a farmer's smock nodded at them. "Well, monsieur?''

Harry scanned the bearded old man. "Not bad, Pastoral.''

"Ah," said Pastoral, "but you knew me.''

"Well, I know you here, but in a different context—in a small village, for instance, you'd fool me for sure.''

"You agree, Miss Barr?''

"Absolutely, Jean-Pierre.''

"Good, good."

"No problems thus far?" asked Harry.

"Not a one." He shut the door.

"Likes to try out his disguises on me," explained Harry.

"So I assumed."

"Otherwise he's a pretty good police detective."

"Going to put him on your list?"

"Nope. But I still think maybe I ought to add Pennoyer's name."

Chapter 10

At one A.M., nearly a half hour after they'd crossed the border and entered Urbania, Harry was sitting alone in his compartment. The shade on the outside door was still up and he was watching the black hill country roll by.

Thunder and lightning had commenced at midnight and in the sizzling blue flashes he caught glimpses of thick forest and sharply slanting ground.

"Maybe I should've told her the truth," he said to himself. "But the fewer people who—"

A faint tapping sounded on the corridor door.

"What?"

"Having a devil of a time getting to sleep amid all this impressive natural phenomenon." Pennoyer opened the door and smiled a toothy smile in at him. "Thought if you were still up we might have a bit of a powwow."

"Sure." Harry took out his pocket watch. "I was going to check on you soon anyway. Come on in."

Pennoyer crossed the threshold, chuckling behind his hand. "All part of the thorough Challenge International Detective Agency service."

"Then at 2:00 A.M. I have to go through the whole train."

Sitting opposite him, the young man said, "Been a very uneventful trip so far. Thanks to you and all these efficient frog chaps."

"We're still not in Kaltzonburg."

"You actually believe, old man, that someone might try to snatch the ruddy obelisk right off this train?"

"Yep, that's one possibility."

"Thing weighs quite a bit. I mean to say, it's no match for Cleo's Needle, but one can't tote it around over one's shoulder."

"Even so."

Casually Pennoyer turned toward the window. When lightning next flashed, he gasped. His monocle fell from his eye and he gasped. "Jove, it's a giant bat!"

Harry swung his head around. "Where?"

It was exactly then that Pennoyer hit him behind the ear, very expertly and very hard with a blackjack.

Harry tumbled from the seat and slumped against the door.

The young man hit him again. "Dreadfully sorry, old man, but we can't have any ace sleuthhounds aboard from this point on."

The door opened and Harry was given a strong push.

He felt as though he were flying clear of the roaring train. He sailed across the blackness, the rain hitting at him as he soared.

Then he hit the ground. Shoulder, ribs, thigh smashing into the slanting hillside.

He heard distant thunder and passed into unconsciousness.

Jennie hadn't undressed. She'd been sitting in her compartment reading a Tauchnitz paper-covered edition of Rider Haggard's *The Wizard* and, soon after the special train had halted at the rain-swept border station, had fallen asleep in her seat.

When the train came to a sudden stop at 2:00 A.M., the novel fell from her lap and hit the carpeted floor with a thud.

She sat up. "What the heck's going on?" She reached to pull up the shade.

"Don't do that, old girl. The fewer of our blokes you get a gander at the better."

Pennoyer had come into her compartment unannounced and uninvited. He held a .32 revolver pointed at the reporter.

"So Harry was right about you."

"Did the chap suspect I was a rotter from the start?"

"He figured no one could be as big an idiot as you appear to be."

Pennoyer chuckled behind his free hand. "Very perceptive bloke," he said. "Proving yet again how wise I was to get rid of him."

She inhaled sharply, standing. "If you've killed Harry I'll— "

"Spare me your wrath, old girl. I doubt he's dead."

"What did you—"

"Was very humane, actually. Merely tapped him on the skull and flung him from his compartment."

"He's hurt then. You—"

"Yes, I suppose one doesn't fall from a moving train onto a mountainside without suffering some damage. Still, don't you know, I gave him a fighting chance. Better than the bullet in the head my superiors suggested." He poked at the air between them with the barrel of his gun. "Now gather up your belongings and be quick about it. And don't even consider trying to get the better of me."

"Why are—"

"This train, do you see, is going to vanish. Soon as we get the bloody obelisk unloaded," he explained. "Unless you wish to vanish with it, Miss Barr, you'll allow me to escort you outside."

The Great Lorenzo's command performance for Prince Rudolph and an audience of Kaltzonburg's most distinguished citizens had been a triumph. He had astounded and enthralled them with such awesome illusions as the Magic Kettle, the Astral Hand and the Floating Lady. Those he'd followed with his bullet catching act, and for an encore he'd introduced his newest trick, the Vanishing Mummy.

Early on the morning after, he sat up abruptly in bed, clutching at his chest. "Harry's been hurt," he said aloud.

The plump, raven-haired lady beneath the silken sheets with him stirred. "Is something troubling you, my adored one?"

"He's lying in the woods beside the railroad tracks . . . six miles outside of . . . Is there a town named Schamgefuhl in this delightful country of yours, Countess Irene, my pet?"

The middle-aged countess rolled over on her ample back. "Whatever are you chattering about, dearest Lolo?"

Swinging free of the wide fourposter, he hurried to the purple ottoman on which he'd neatly stacked his clothes the night before. "Schamgefuhl . . . I see a sign bearing that melodious name. Is there such a place?"

"Well, yes, Lolo, but no one goes there anymore," she answered. "The spa is quite out of fashion and the only people who'd be seen—"

"Where is it, my pudding?"

"A good three hundred miles to the south, Lolo, not far from the border. Why are you—"

"I must use your telephone at once."

"To call someone in Schamgefuhl? I doubt they have the telephone service in such a backward—"

"No, to contact my dear friend and generous patron, Prince Rudy." He was nearly dressed, struggling with his final shirt stud. "He's going to have to convince the police and the railroad officials that I'm not a lunatic and that my vision is anything more than a hallucination. Yes, I am going to need considerable cooperation to get to Harry."

"Who is this Harry person?"

"An old friend."

"He is in trouble in, of all places, Schamgefuhl?"

"I'm not getting a perfectly clear picture. It's possible he's broken his neck."

When she sighed the pale blue sheets shivered and whispered. ''Such loyalty you display, Lolo, such touching samaritanism. Yet another reason why I am so passionately fond of you,'' she said, smiling over the top of the sheet at him, ''If, however, this dear friend of yours already has broken his neck, there may not be all that much need to rush.''

''I am hoping, dear one, part of my vision is in error.'' Fastening his cloak around his shoulders, the Great Lorenzo went striding from the early morning bedchamber.

Chapter 11

Harry opened his eyes.

He was flat on his back in the middle of an off-white hospital room.

The early afternoon sun showed over the rooftops of the buildings outside his high window.

"Okay," he told himself, "I'm not in the woods any longer."

His ribs, the ones on his right side, hurt. A fine, intense sort of pain it was. And his side was tightly bandaged.

When he reached to scratch at the bandages, he discovered that his right wrist and part of his right hand were encased in a heavy cast.

The off-white door opened and a very young doctor came shyly in. "Good afternoon, Herr Challenge," he said in his pale voice. "We are awake, I see."

"Apparently."

"I will," said the lean, fair-haired doctor, "explain to you where you are and what has happened, should you be anxious to know."

"That would liven things up, yes."

"First, however," he said as he approached the bed, "allow me to ask you if a cablegram from your loving father would unduly upset you?"

"It wouldn't."

"I have such here." From a lumpy pocket of his white

smock he took a tongue depressor, a bottle of yellow pills and an envelope. "I may open it for you, since your hand is not able?"

"Appreciate that."

"I am, by the way, Herr Doctor Hauser." He placed the message, carefully, in Harry's bruised left hand.

His father said:

> *Dear Son: Quit malingering. We have another case. Scatterbrained young woman named Stowe will contact you in Kaltzonburg. Claims her crackpot parent is missing. Big fee. Get up and get cracking. Your loving father, the Challenge International Detective Agency.*

Harry said, "She must be Professor Stowe's daughter."

"Beg pardon?"

"Never mind. Just explain to me what the situation is."

"It is a most unusual case," Dr. Hauser began. "Not from a medical standpoint. There we have nothing very unusual—fractured wrist, three fractured ribs, bruises, abrasions and a mild concussion. Exactly what's to be expected with someone who's been thrown from a moving train."

"You get many patients here who've been tossed off trains?"

"Well, in fact, no. You are my first, but then I am only a full-fledged doctor six and one half months."

"This hospital is . . . where?"

"You are in Kaltzonburg, as a guest of no less a personage than Prince Rudolph himself."

Using the elbow of his good arm, Harry worked into a sitting position in bed. "The train I was on . . . did it get through okay?"

The young doctor coughed discreetly. "Everyone is being very secretive," he confided. "It is my impression, though, that this particular train has vanished."

"What do you mean?"

"It never arrived at its destination. There is no trace of it," he replied. "At least, so I hear."

"But Jennie . . . everyone else on the damn train . . . what happened to them?"

"They apparently disappeared along with it," said Dr. Hauser. "Let us perhaps change the topic of conversation, since you seem to be getting overly—"

"No, damn it. I have to find out what happened to Jennie." He attempted to get out of bed. "That wasn't even the real obelisk."

"You must not try to—"

The room became all at once smaller and greyer and it closed in on Harry. He passed out.

Fully dressed and fairly wobbly, Harry eased out of his hospital room. He'd been waiting at a crack in the door for the past five minutes, watching. The off-white corridor was empty now.

Unsteady on his feet, he started down the hallway. He'd noticed, while doing his reconnoitering, a door labeled STAIRWAY to his right.

The day had ended and the gaslights along the hall were on. The single narrow window showed him a rectangle of bright-lit public square ringed by shops and cafés far below.

Harry was three paces beyond the window when a hand caught hold of his left arm.

"If you must go for a twilight stroll, my boy, allow me to assist you."

"Lorenzo," said Harry. "How did you manage to sneak—"

"I never sneak," the portly magician reminded him. "Being highly esteemed in royal circles, I have full access to the Kaltzonburg Memorial Hospital, which was founded by Prince Rudy's great uncle. I was about to peek in on you when—"

"Listen, I have to get the hell out of here," Harry explained. "Jennie's in trouble . . . someplace."

"She and a squad of Paris' finest, plus an obelisk, are missing."

"That's not even the real obelisk."

The Great Lorenzo nodded as he opened the stairwell door. "Yes, I understand you and Inspector Swann worked a variation of my famed Chinese Tomb illusion and switched obelisks."

"The one on the special train was made out of *papier-mâché*. The real one, with Swann riding shotgun, traveled here in the baggage car of the regular Paris-Kaltzonburg Express in a big crate marked Farm Implements." Harry hesitated at the top of the stairwell. "How many floors?"

"Six. Would you rather I spirit you into a lift. I'm very good at diverting attention from—"

"Nope, I don't want to risk getting stopped."

"Might an old and trusted comrade mention, Harry my lad, that you look godawful."

"Yep, seems to happen every time I get sapped and dumped off a train." He took a deep breath and, with the Great Lorenzo supporting him, began his descent of the metal steps. "Did the real obelisk get through?"

"Unharmed. The gewgaw was delivered, by the estimable Inspector Swann, to the château of Baron Groll. That was two days ago and since then there's been not—"

"Two days?" Harry halted. "No, it couldn't have arrived until this morning because . . . Christ. I forgot to ask Dr. Hauser how long I've been here."

"This is the eve of your second day, my boy. You were out cold for a good long while." The magician was watching him closely. "Harry, might it not be better to rest at least one more night before—"

"Nope, no." He resumed his downward climb. "Jennie's been missing for two days."

"Inspector Swann is, with the help and cooperation of the Urbanian police, making a thorough and detailed—"

"You sound like a police department handout, Lorenzo. Two days and nothing is what it comes to."

The magician was panting now. "Not that I expected, oh, an illuminated scroll or even a small pewter loving cup," he said. "Yet, after pulling strings, cutting red tape, moving heaven and earth to retrieve your pitiful broken body from the flinders at the side of the—"

"That's how they knew where I was. You had a vision." Harry halted again. "Sorry, I didn't think to ask about that."

"One more proof, lad, that you're not at your usual level of performance," the Great Lorenzo pointed out as they continued their downward course. "An injury to the head can do that. Well do I recall a time in Istanbul when I was conked on the coco by an Indian club being wielded by the irate husband of a voluptuous lady bareback rider who managed to look always graceful even though she weighed in at over—"

"Whatever shape my brain is in," said Harry, "I have to start looking for Jennie. Damn it, I didn't even tell her we were just decoys. She thinks the obelisk is the real thing."

"It has been my experience that true love—something, alas, I have enjoyed but seldom in my long and colorful life—true love makes for a certain amount of truth telling and confiding, Harry."

"I know." They'd reached the fourth floor of the hospital and he paused for a moment. "The thing is, Lorenzo, I guess I'm still not absolutely sure I can trust Jennie. While we were traveling from Paris to Zevenburg I was certain . . . then it turned out she was trailing me to get material for her damn newspaper articles."

Tapping his temple, the magician said, "The poor child was under the influence of that most wicked of gentlemen, the infamous Max Orchardson. You can't really blame her for what she did while in a state of—"

"I haven't figured out how much of what she did is due to being hypnotized and how much . . . Hell, what differ-

ence does it make? I have to find her.'' He started
downward.

The music of an accordian drifted out of a sidewalk café
across the square. The tune reminded Harry of one he and
Jennie had heard on the floating restaurant on the Seine.
''What?''

The Great Lorenzo, who still held Harry's arm while
they walked across the parklike square, said, ''I was men-
tioning that a very handsome young woman named
Belphoebe Stowe has been to the hospital to try to visit
you. On several occasions. She brought a basket of very
tasty hothouse plums on her second attempt.''

''My father put her on to me.'' They were passing an
empty wrought iron bench. ''Think I'd like to sit for a
spell.''

After helping Harry to do that, the magician settled
down beside him. ''Perhaps we ought to consult a private
physician before you go off on—''

''I'll be okay. A shade shaky is all.''

''Miss Stowe is a wholesome British lass, blonde and
well formed. A trifle on the slender side for my taste,''
said the Great Lorenzo. ''Reminds me of a lady-in-waiting
I once sawed in half while touring Bosnia in the spring
of—''

''I don't want any new clients just yet.''

''Your dear papa assumes this case has concluded. You
have, after all, put an end to the haunting of the musée.
You have delivered the authentic obelisk safely to the arms
of its new rightful owner. All's well, my boy.''

''And where's Jennie?''

''Ah, but being a practical gent with the heart and soul
of an accountant, your father doesn't see—''

''I won't take on anything new until I find Jennie.'' He
tried to scratch at his side with the hand that wore the cast.
''Damn, I'm going to have trouble even using a gun.''

''One more reason for being prudent.'' The magician

poked at the grass with the brightly polished toe of his shoe. "While sharing a plum or two with the handsome and deeply distraught Miss Stowe, I did establish that she is the one and only daughter of the illustrious Professor G. P. R. Stowe."

"Yep, the guy who built that flying machine."

"None other. Seems the scholarly old gentleman disappeared nearly a year ago." He plucked a lit cigarette from the night air, took a single puff and vanished it. "Miss Stowe, whose handsome bosom is filled with anguish and who has an independent income that is most impressive, has reason to believe her long lost parent may be in Urbania."

"What reason?"

"She did not confide that little tidbit in me."

"Right now, even if Professor Stowe is in cahoots with Orchardson, I can't . . . Hold on." Harry got, not very steadily, to his feet. He started fumbling under his coat with his left hand.

A stocky figure had moved out from behind a dead marble fountain and was crossing the darkness toward them. "It is only I, M. Challenge."

Harry remained standing there. "Have you found out anything about Jennie Barr, Inspector Swann."

"I was just now on my way to the hospital to consult with you when I noted you and your loyal friend resting here." The French police inspector took off his dark bowler hat and held it with both hands over the middle buttons of his thick overcoat. "You are well enough to be up and about, monsieur?"

"Just about. What have you found out?"

Swann's thick moustache drooped. "We have this very afternoon located the special train," he said. "It had been cleverly switched off onto a disused spur line."

"What about Jennie and the others?"

Swann lowered his head. "The train, monsieur, has been located at the bottom of a deep lake at the end of the tracks,'' he said slowly. "Until we are able to do some diving, we must assume that all who were aboard are drowned.''

Harry did something he'd only done twice before in his life. He fainted.

Chapter 12

Harry circled the rough-hewn wooden table. The table nearly filled the vine covered arbor next to the hillside cottage the Great Lorenzo had brought him to last night.

Spread out atop it were several of the ordinance maps Inspector Swann had loaned him. Resting his sore backside against the table edge, Harry traced his good forefinger along another of the probable routes the hijackers could've taken after running the special train into the lake.

"Lake Knochen." He looked away from the map, out from the arbor. The spires of Kaltzonburg were still blurred with morning mist far downhill. "Jennie's not dead."

"Scat!" came the voice of the Great Lorenzo from within the cottage. "Begone."

Harry sat down on one of the benches, studying a map and absently rubbing his cast.

From around the side of the whitewashed stone cottage came the magician. "Have you ever awakened from an uneasy night's sleep to find an obese calico cat sleeping on your chest?" he inquired.

"Once, in Estonia."

"No wonder I was dreaming I'd become Santa Claus." He wore an impressive dressing gown that was covered with realistic depictions of gigantic orange and black tropical flowers. "You're looking much more chipper this morning, my boy."

"Not quite up to chipper yet, but getting close." From the arbor you would see part of the winding dirt road, a quarter mile off, that climbed their hillside. A leathery old farmer was urging a half dozen shaggy goats downhill. "About my fainting last night. I—"

"Think nothing of it." The Great Lorenzo seated himself on another of the wooden benches. "I've swooned a few times myself. The initial instance I can clearly recall took place during my vanished youth and involved my seeing, in a nearly undraped state, the first tattooed lady I had ever . . . Are you in the mood for breakfast?"

"Not very hungry."

"Coffee then?"

"That'd be fine."

"Haven't tried this particular magic word for many a moon. Let us see if it's still efficacious." He lifted up one of the big maps and slid a plump hand under it. "Presto!"

The hand reappeared holding a steaming mug of coffee.

Taking it, Harry grinned. "Suppose I had asked for breakfast?"

"Presto." From beneath the map he produced a china plate holding a fat, many-layered pastry. "Shame to waste this, now I've conjured it up." From behind his left ear he plucked a silver fork. "Enough sugar in your coffee, my boy?"

Harry sampled it and nodded.

The Great Lorenzo concentrated on the pastry, which was rich in various kinds of chocolate filling and topped with thick whipped cream, for the next few minutes. He ate and watched the reluctant goats make their way out of sight around a quirk in the road.

"There are," said Harry finally, tapping the map he'd been studying, "at least two routes they could've taken away from the lake. See here? Around this way you pick up a good road just over these hills. That eventually takes you to this highway. Or they could've gone back across the railroad tracks right at this point, moved down through the valley here. Beyond that you connect with another fair highway.''

"We have to assume they didn't know they weren't going to be stealing the real obelisk." The magician licked a dab of chocolate off his thumb. "The real thing weighs a couple of tons, does it not?''

"Nearer to three.''

"You don't simply cry out, 'All right, lads, everyone lift with a will and off we go.' What's needed is a method of draying the thing," he pointed out.

"Right, they had to have a wagon, a damn sturdy one, waiting there at the lake for them.''

"Large wagon, pulled by a strong team of horses. That has to leave a trail, even without a granite keepsake aboard.''

"Inspector Swann and the local police are supposed to be working on that, looking for wagon tracks and all," Harry said. "First, though, he's concentrating on getting divers down to . . . Damn it, Lorenzo. She can't be dead." He hit the table with his cast, winced.

"She's not.''

Harry frowned across at him. "Have you had some sort of vision about—''

"Alas, no. Merely a hunch." He lifted the map again, peered under it. "Dare I have another pastry? No, only a cruller this time. Presto.''

Harry waited until the magician had taken a few appreciative bits of the freshly materialized frosted cruller. "You can't control the visions? Concentrate on Jennie and see—''

"Unfortunately my gift does not work that way, Harry. Over the years I've experimented with varied and sundry ways of trying to . . .'' He grimaced suddenly, his fingers tightening on the cruller until it broke into crumbly pieces. Rocking sideways on his bench, the Great Lorenzo started producing a low moaning.

"Lorenzo?" Harry jumped up, ran around the table.

"I'm fine . . . stay back . . .'' He pressed both hands to his chest, continuing to moan. "She is . . . alive . . .

Jennie's alive . . . I can see . . . a castle . . . like a Gothic ruin . . . same castle I saw before . . . with all of us in it . . . Jennie is . . . locked in a . . . stone room . . . young man taunting her . . . nasty fellow . . . monocle . . .''

"Bertie Pennoyer," muttered Harry.

"I see . . . evil old man . . . decaying . . . Zaytoon . . . It's Anwar Zaytoon . . . another woman . . . more dangerous than he . . . dark and beautiful . . . Why, it's . . .'' His body jerked, shivered.

Harry carefully sat on the bench beside his friend. He put his good arm around his shoulders. "Easy now."

The Great Lorenzo began to breathe regularly again. "Some of them get rough, like climbing an alp or two." His plump face was blurred with perspiration. He concentrated on breathing in and out for a while.

"So Jennie is okay?"

"Appeared a bit peckish. Also pale and weary. Otherwise alive and not seriously injured."

"And Zaytoon's the one who's got her."

"He is the master of the picturesque castle I saw, yes. Along with this Pennoyer fellow you mentioned."

"Pennoyer is the amiable gent who conked me and treated me like a sack of mail," said Harry. "But you saw someone else at the castle."

The magician took up a fragment of his ruined cruller between thumb and forefinger and contemplated it. "Only a fleeting glimpse I had of the lady," he said. "I am certain, however, she is the one we met before and quite recently."

"Not Naida Strand?"

" 'Tis she and none other."

"Damn, we left her at Blackwood Castle in Orlandia, sleeping in her coffin."

"Same as any other true vampire." The Great Lorenzo shrugged. "We both had the opportunity to drive a stake through her black heart. Too sentimental by far we were."

"I don't think I can kill anyone that way. Certainly not a woman."

"Nor I. Whenever I see a sleeping lady, be she vampire and sorceress most foul or sweet-souled maiden, slaying her is the furthest thought from my mind." He spread his hands wide. "Which is why, dear lad, we now have her to contend with as well as the rest of this nest of blackguards."

"Worse, Jennie has to contend with her." Harry tapped the nearest map. "What about the location of Zaytoon's castle?"

"These visions vary." He coughed into his hand. "Sometimes I get the exact location, down to the street address. Other times I don't. This time I didn't. Zaytoon's castle is somewhere in Urbania and that's the closest I can come."

From the misty courtyard came the harsh chatter of machine-gun fire.

Jennie Barr was sitting on the cot, her notebook open on her lap.

Zaytoon testing weapons again today, she wrote. *Demonstrating to potential customers?*

In order to see out the only window in the small grey stone room, Jennie had to stand atop the rickety cot. The view afforded by the effort was not especially inspiring. All she was able to see was another turret of the bleak castle she was imprisoned in and a thin slice of sky. The activities down in the courtyard she had to guess at, assisted by the sounds the various weapons—machine guns, rifles, grenades—made and occasional puffs of smoke that drifted across her portion of sky.

The morning was a pale, overcast one. Jennie'd determined that soon after awakening nearly an hour ago.

She bit on the end of her stubby pencil, glancing up at the slot of a window.

When she began writing again, she put down *Is Harry alive?*

She'd written that line before, several times since she'd

been a prisoner of Anwar Zaytoon, and she hadn't meant to put it on paper again.

"He must be alive and he'll find me sooner or later," she said to herself. "But if he doesn't, I've got to keep working on a way to get myself—"

The thick metal door of her room rattled, made its usual rasping sound and swung open inward.

"Top of the morning, old girl." Bertie Pennoyer came briskly in, a tray in one hand. "One hopes, don't you know, that your appetite's improved. You keep up this ruddy fasting and you'll— "

"I want to see Zaytoon."

Pennoyer kicked the heavy door shut with his heel. "Quite out of the question, as I've been telling you." He set the tray on the stone floor next to her cot.

"He's holding me prisoner and I want to—"

"You're a guest." Pennoyer was wearing a double-breasted navy blue blazer and white trousers. Leaning back against the wall, he popped his monocle and commenced polishing it against his sleeve. "You'll remain our guest, don't you see, until you decide to be talkative."

"I'll talk only to Zaytoon."

"Stubborn, ain't you?" He held the monocle toward the lone window, squinting. "Our jovial host, the guv as I call him, is a bit under the weather still. Only to be expected with a gent as far along in years as the guv is. What strength he's got, he has to reserve for the many business affairs—"

"How old is he exactly?" asked Jennie. "When I dug into his background once, I couldn't find any evidence of when or where he'd been born."

"The guv's quite long in the tooth, but I've never had a gander at his birth certificate." Pennoyer covered his mouth with the hand holding his monocle and chuckled. "Afraid, old girl, I can't give you any facts to scribble in your memory book."

She said, "I came across a rumor once that Zaytoon

wasn't born in the nineteenth century at all. They said that by some magical means he's—''

Pennoyer's monocle dropped to the stones and cracked down the middle. ''Bally old wives' tale and nothing more.'' Bending from the waist, he gathered up the pieces. ''One hears far too much ridiculous nonsense being nattered about. A reporter of your reputation, one would think, is above believing such poppycock.''

''If he is, say, a few hundred years old,'' persisted Jennie, ''then he has a darn good reason for wanting the obelisk and the secret of eternal life. Could be the methods he's been using aren't working any—''

''Who the ruddy devil told you that?'' He squared his shoulders and glared at her. ''Speaking of the obelisk, which the guv is interested in purely from a collector's point of view—we've been deuced patient with you, don't you know. Now the time has come to be open with us.''

''I'll tell Zaytoon himself, face to face.''

He came closer. ''Thus far, dear girl, the guv's been too busy with other affairs to take a hand in questioning you,'' he said. ''Maybe you haven't realized that this snuggery of yours is deuced close to some of the old torture chambers. If you aren't more forthcoming about where the rascal obelisk has gotten to by nightfall, then you may pay those chambers a bit of a visit.''

''I'd be happy to talk to Zaytoon right now.''

Pennoyer leaned. ''A lovely old friend of yours has joined forces with us recently and is, at this very moment, a guest of the castle,'' he said. ''She tells me she's most anxious to join in questioning you. And she'll, don't you know, be doing that tonight unless you come clean. Her name is Naida Strand.''

Jennie blinked. ''I thought she perished in Blackwood Castle.''

''Far from it. She's very much alive,'' he assured her. ''Well, as alive as a full-fledged vampire can be.''

*   *   *

Harry spotted the approaching cyclist first. It was less than fifteen minutes after the Great Lorenzo's vision and the magician was hunched, elbows on table, scanning an ordinance map. "Perhaps the name of a town, a river, a lake will trigger something."

Glancing downhill, Harry noted a bright scarlet cycle being peddled energetically in their direction. "What did you say Professor Stowe's daughter looked like?"

"Belphoebe Stowe is a healthy, out-of-doors sort of young lady. Typical product of an upper-class British up-bringing and the sort of woman who's helped make the empire great."

"Blonde?"

"Blonde, yes. Tall, close to five foot nine I'd estimate. Tends toward the slim, yet—"

"She's coming up the hill right now. Dressed in a riding habit."

"On horseback?"

"On a bicycle."

The Great Lorenzo finally looked up from the map, narrowing his eyes. "Yes, that's she. Sits a cycle well, doesn't she?"

"How does Belphoebe Stowe happen to know I'm staying in this cottage you borrowed from your duchess?"

"Countess."

"Countess then. How?"

"Inspector Swann is aware of the location, as is Countess Irene." Standing up, he brushed crumbs from his front and retied the orange sash of his dressing gown.

The cyclist disappeared from view, hidden by the cottage itself, and a moment later there was a forceful knocking upon the front door.

"Would you mind scooting around and welcoming the young lady, Harry? I hate to play host when dressed so casually."

"Anybody who greeted me wearing a thing like that'd make a terrific impression." Reluctantly he left the arbor, walked across the tree-filled yard to the front of the place.

Belphoebe Stowe, wearing white riding britches, a black jacket and riding boots, was about to resume knocking when she noticed Harry. "You would be Mr. Harry Challenge?"

"I would," he admitted, "and you're Belphoebe Stowe. Let me save us some time by explaining that—"

"My father has been kidnapped again." She came hurrying along the flagstone path to him.

"Again? I wasn't aware he'd even been—"

"In the first instance, it was a gross and, I suspect, effete, man named Max Orchardson. Most recently Anwar Zaytoon, often alluded to as the Merchant of Death by the more sensation-minded journalists of the day, has abducted him," she explained. "My father, although quite brilliant and inventive in a rather strange and eccentric way, is not an especially admirable nor particularly likeable man. He is, as I find I must keep reminding myself, my only living parent. I, as fate would have it, am his only child. It is my duty, therefore, to rescue him from the clutches of Zaytoon."

"I'd like to be able to—"

"What I shall require from you, Mr. Challenge, is your strong right arm to . . . Ah, but do forgive me. I note, as I should have at once were I not so preoccupied with my own affairs, your right arm is injured. You will, since you seem a bright and perceptive man, no doubt appreciate the meaning of my metaphor. What I need is a stalwart and fearless champion to come with me to this castle where Zaytoon holds my improvident father. Someone to handle any hand to hand—"

"Whoa," suggested Harry. "By coincidence, we were just talking about the castle. Thing is, we're not certain where it's located. Do you—"

"Well, of course, I know where it is. Have I not been devoting the past week to locating it? Ever since this rather vulgar postcard reached me in my hotel in Rome, after having followed me halfway around the globe. My father, you see, has no idea I have been devoting my waking hours, along with a considerable amount of my own money, to—''

"May I see the postcard?"

"Certainly you can. Being a detective, you will quite naturally wish to examine it thoroughly. I can save you some time by explaining in advance that my father, apparently having to sneak this missive out to me, had no time to put in many specifics." She undid the three top buttons of her silk blouse, dipped in two fingers and extracted the card. "Please ignore the shamelessly underdressed young woman on the front of it. I am giving my father the benefit of the doubt and assuming he, being rushed and in fear of his life, had little choice as to what sort of postcard he could post to me."

The picture side showed a plump young woman in a very thin gown as she rose on her tiptoes to greet the newly risen moon. On the other side, in a crabbed hand, was the message:

> *Now Z. has taken me from O. Do try to help. This is more than I can stand. I am . . . must go now. In haste, your loving father, GPR Stowe.*

Seven weeks ago the card had been posted in the town of Lowen. Harry knew, having spent some time going over maps of most of Urbania, that the town was only twenty miles from here.

"As I mentioned, Mr. Challenge, I have been able, after discreetly making inquiries in Lowen, to locate this castle which Zaytoon and his coterie have rented for the season," said Belphoebe. "While I am an expert shot and excell at most sports, I am still a woman. Thus it was I contacted your father, whose admirable reputation I have long been familiar with, to inquire if he had an able-bodied operative anywhere in this part of Europe. I was pleased, it goes without saying, when I received a cable informing me that his own son was right here in Urbania. Are you, by the way, an only child?"

"I am, yes."

"Then there is something we have in common. I find, and no doubt you will agree, that some degree of common interest is often a sound basis for a friendship," she told him. "When will you be able to undertake my case?"

He drew out his pocket watch. "I'm ready now."

"I like that," she told him. "No nonsense, right to business. We will get along famously, Mr. Challenge."

"Never doubted it."

Chapter 13

"I wonder," requested Belphoebe, "if you gentlemen might refrain from smoking those odorous cigars."

The Great Lorenzo was sitting opposite her in the plush-lined coach. "Ah, but of course. Forgive me for assaulting your delicate nostrils." He passed his plump hand in front of the smoldering stogie and it vanished.

Harry, who was sharing a seat with the blonde young woman, got rid of his cigar by tossing it out the open window of the borrowed coach that was carrying them through the afternoon to the town of Lowen.

"One's nostrils do not have to be especially sensitive to be offended by such a vile stench."

"Suppose," said Harry, "you give us a few more details about your father."

"My father is a brilliant experimenter in the field of heavier-than-air flight," she said. "He is, as well, a profligate and totally unbridled old reprobate."

Harry nodded, watching the woodlands they were rushing through. "How did Max Orchardson come to kidnap him in the first place?"

"Initially my lamentable father made the acquaintance of Orchardson at some disreputable soirée in some foul backwater of London," she replied. "Father, along with his multitude of other faults and foibles, believes himself to be interested in things occult and supernatural. An interest that is, as you know, shared by the awful Orchardson. He made the mistake of confiding the results of his work with flying machines to that loathsome man. My father really has made incredible strides in the designing and building of such mechanisms. He is far and away ahead of such men as Professor S. P. Langley of your own country.''

"These giant bats are really your father's aerodromes?''

"I am afraid they are, Mr. Challenge.'' She sighed, unbuttoning the lace-trimmed blouse she had changed into before they'd commenced their journey. She reached inside. "If you will but peruse these plans you will note all the modifications called for by Orchardson.''

Accepting the three sheets of flimsy paper, Harry unfolded them and spread them out on his knee. "How'd you come by these?''

"They are copies I made unbeknowst to my misguided father,'' she answered. "Originally, you see, Orchardson pretended he was only interested in financing the building of more aerodromes.'' She twisted the topmost button of her blouse. "My gullible, and not always sober, father willingly moved into an estate of Orchardson's, a dreary pile in the wilds of Barsetshire. After a few scant months it became all too evident the man had other things in mind.''

The Great Lorenzo leaned, scanning the plans upside down. "The demonstration we had, my dear, gave us the impression these mechanical creatures can be controlled.''

She nodded. "That is another of my father's inventions,'' Belphoebe said. "By utilizing an advanced electrical system, one I confess I do not fully understand, he has been able to make an aerodrome do his bidding. Goaded by Orchardson, my detestable father developed a flying machine that could be made to do any number of vile things.''

"They can pick up people in their claws? Push them off high places and—''

"All that and more,'' she confirmed. "When my way-

ward father showed me the plans you now are studying
copies of, Mr. Challenge, I knew at once that Orchardson
was much more than a patron of science.''

"You talked your father into quitting?''

"I did, a task that required all my wiles and wits," she
said. "Orchardson, however, was not to be so easily
thwarted. Once he realized my father had left him and
returned to his own home, he dispatched his minions to
abduct him. This they succeeded in doing, after rendering
me unconscious with a rare Brazilian drug. Upon awakening, two weeks later, I set out to follow what was, by
then, a cold trail. Even so, I was able to pick up clues as
to where they had taken my father. Orchardson has immense wealth—some say he has found the lost secret of
transforming base metal to gold—and thus he has been
able to lead me a merry chase from England to Egypt to
Ruritania to Albania to Italy. It was while in Rome, where
I arrived a few weeks after the wicked Orchardson had
again moved his base of operations, that I received the
bawdy postcard that led me to call upon your capable
father for assistance.''

"How did Zaytoon get hold of him?''

"Of that I have no knowledge. Zaytoon and Orchardson
are archrivals, which must be why my father has become a
pawn in some dread game they are playing.''

The Great Lorenzo reached up over his head to pluck an
eclair out of the shadows. "I trust the scent of chocolate
will not offend you, Miss Stowe?''

"Not at all," she assured him.

The Great Lorenzo came limping into Harry's room at
the Lion's Paw Inn. "The dear countess was right," he
remarked. "This quaint little town has fallen on sad times.''

Harry was at the cracked window, looking out across
the tile rooftops toward the wooded hills. "That must be
Gewunden Castle up yonder," he said. "Big place with a
high stone wall surrounding it.''

The portly magician limped over to him. "Yes, my boy, that's the very pile I saw in my recent vision. Jennie is within its gloomy confines at this very moment."

"Why are you still limping?" Harry turned his back on the window, sat on the edge of a sagging Morris chair.

"I am supposedly suffering from the gout, remember?" He pulled a cigar out of the air. "Join me?"

"Think I'll cut down."

"Ah, the prim Miss Stowe has had an effect on your—"

"The gout business is to fool the folks at the inn," Harry pointed out. "To convince one and all you've come to Lowen to take advantage of the hot springs. We're your concerned nephew and niece."

After puffing on the cigar and limping back and forth across the threadbare carpet, the Great Lorenzo said, "A dedicated performer, my boy, never lets down. I am supposed to be suffering with the gout and as long as we're here in this ragtag watering place I intend to limp in a most convincing and pitiable manner."

Harry grinned. "You are convincing," he said. "Brings tears to my eyes just watching you."

"I dropped in, now that we're all settled, to announce that I am going out to hobble through the lanes and alleys of the town," he said. "My task will be to gather in all the information and intelligence I can regarding the Zaytoon household." He limped toward the off-kilter door. "We'll meet, as planned, in the cheerless dining room of this hostelry when twilight descends."

"Yep, that'll give Belphoebe and I time to take a closer look at the castle."

The Great Lorenzo held up a cautionary forefinger. "Be extremely careful while you're in the vicinity of that place, Harry."

"You giving me the benefit of another vision?"

"Merely the benefit of common sense." He bowed, opened the door and limped out into the shabby corridor.

Chapter 14

Belphoebe spread her arms wide and took an enthusiastic deep breath. "This has been quite invigorating thus far," she said happily. "One can see why you so enjoy the detective profession, Mr. Challenge. For it provides both an intellectual challenge and the opportunity for a satisfying amount of healthful outdoor exercise."

Harry wiped his forehead with his pocket handkerchief. "Yes, a ten mile hike up the side of a thickly forested steep hill is great fun," he said. "Sometimes, when I'm between cases, I do this sort of thing for the sheer joy of it."

Smiling, she said, "You have a rather pleasant sense of humor."

He moved ahead through the oak trees until he reached the edge of a small clearing. About a half mile uphill loomed Gewunden Castle. From his coat pocket he took a small pair of opera glasses. "Ugly joint."

The thick stone walls were a good ten feet high, topped with rusty spikes and what looked to be jagged shards of broken bottle glass. The castle itself was a complex cluster of towers and dark tile roofs.

Belphoebe came up beside him. She undid the top buttons of her blouse. "I have brought a sketching pad and a suitable pencil," she told him. "I am quite good at drawing landscapes and buildings, much in the manner of your Joseph Pennell."

"What we could really use is a floor plan of the damn place," he said. "Nobody in town has one, though."

"An accurate rendering of the exterior will enable us to make certain speculations as to what lies within."

"Okay. I want all the gates and doorways marked down," Harry told her. "And a rough sketch of the whole setup."

"That I can assuredly supply," said the blonde Belphoebe. "If I might borrow your glasses for a moment."

"Sure, here."

"I made a few sketches on my earlier visit." She put the binoculars to her eyes. "Yet I dared not approach anywhere near this close."

Harry frowned, his shoulders hunching slightly. As the young woman began making notes on her sketch pad, he backed away.

They hadn't followed a trail up here, and the trees rose high all around them. Branches thick with new leaves were tangled and intertwined overhead and brush grew high on the mossy ground.

Glancing from side to side, Harry walked back along the way they'd come.

Although sunset was at least a good hour off, the day was already starting to fade.

He had a growing feeling that someone was watching them. Eyes narrowed, he looked to the left and right and then up into the treetops.

"I believe I will get a better view from the clearing just below," called Belphoebe.

Harry turned. "Don't get out in the open."

But she was already leaving the shelter of the trees.

He started running. "Belphoebe, stay here."

From above came a flapping, creaking noise—a harsh whirring, and a wheezy coughing.

Then a gigantic mechanical bat swooped down over the clearing.

Belphoebe was aware of it, too, and was trying to get

back to the shelter of the woods from the center of the clearing.

The flying machine dived right for her. Two long, clawed arms swung down from its midsection, snatching at her. The second try was successful and the mechanical bat caught her up by the arm and a shoulder.

Its giant wings flapped at an accelerated rate and they both began rising up from the clearing.

Belphoebe cried out, kicking at the dark-painted aerodrome. Her sketchbook fell from her hand, fluttering down to the ground.

Harry had reached the open area and he was running toward them. If he could leap and catch hold of Belphoebe before she rose out of reach, then he could—

The earth opened beneath his feet. Rotted wood, branches, leaves snapped and he found himself plummeting down into a deep hole.

At exactly five o'clock the clock high in the tower of the Lowen town hall struck the hour. A lifesize automation representing Hercules emerged from his lair, strode along a catwalk and whacked a bronze gong five times with his club.

Before the last echo had died, the carved wooden doors of the rustic little café across the square from the clock tower swung open. Two large swarthy men in the full military uniform of the far-off Latin American country of Panazuela escorted the Great Lorenzo out into the impending dusk. It was a double-time procession and it ended with the magician being deposited in a bed of tulips at the base of a statue of one of the great Urbanian statesmen of the eighteenth century and his equally praiseworthy horse.

"Do not," advised one of the colonels, "be so unwise, senhor, as to give offense to the senhora again."

"In my country," said the Great Lorenzo as he rose up out of the mangled tulips with considerable dignity, "it is not considered offensive to present a lovely lady with a bouquet of—"

"This is not your country, senhor," mentioned the other colonel, "nor is it ours. The Senhora Picada is here on a most important mission for her beloved husband, General Miguel Picada, an extremely able militarist and a man renowned for his jealousy. Were he here, you would be stretched out upon—"

"Gentlemen," said the magician, "my mission is similar to that of the handsome Mrs. Picada. I, too, find myself most interested in the munitions to be obtained from the esteemed Anwar Zaytoon. Thus, when I chanced to overhear her refer to her similar goal, I bethought me that perhaps a merger of our—"

"The next time you approach her with a handful of paper flowers, senhor, we will not be so gracious."

"Those were real roses," he assured them. "Do you think the Great Lorenzo materializes paper—"

"*Adeus,* senhor."

Executing an impressive about-face, they marched side by side back inside the café.

The Great Lorenzo fluffed his side-whiskers. "A *dozen* roses, too," he muttered. "That rarely fails."

"Ah, truly it is written that the monsoon that rips off your roof oft reveals a rainbow in the sky."

"Eh?" The magician did a slow half turn, stepped free of the tulip bed and scrutinized the Chinese gentleman who was sitting on a nearby wooden bench. "Were you razzing me, sir, or passing along a bit of celestial wisdom?"

The man was small and lean, dressed in a frock coat and grey trousers. A top hat rested beside him on the bench. "Wisely it is said that the newly painted barn sometimes fools the homesick cow."

"All well and good, yet . . . Ha!" He took a few steps toward him. "I didn't—you're absolutely right there—recognize you sans your stage finery, old friend."

Standing, the Chinese bowed. "I am no longer a colleague, Lorenzo."

"You mean you have ceased to be Fengjing the Amazing, Master of Oriental Wizardry?"

Fengjing shook his head. "I have found it more lucrative in the employ of a warlord of my native country."

"A shame, since no one does the Caged Dove illusion as deftly as you."

"True." He bowed more deeply. "What is it that has caused our paths to cross?"

"I suspect," said the Great Lorenzo, approaching the bench, "we share an interest in one Anwar Zaytoon."

"It is written that the vulture and the maggot may feast on the same carrion."

"You are in town to buy arms, are you not?"

"I am to call on the esteemed Anwar Zaytoon, or rather on his trusted servitors, this very evening," replied Fengjing. "There is to be a small reception at his rather dour residence. Should you care to gain entrance, oh friend of my former life, it might be arranged for you to become one of my party."

"That would come in very handy," said the magician. "And, if it's not imposing too much, I'll take the liberty of bringing a young associate of mine along."

Chapter 15

Harry fell approximately eleven feet straight down. He managed to land on his good side. The impression he got, when he banged into the stone floor, was that his taped ribs made a harplike twanging sound. That hand that was in the cast jumped up to whap him across the cheekbone.

A rich assortment of broken branches, splintered planking and tangled brush was beneath him and a bit more came drifting down in his wake to land atop him. Several nettles found their way under his collar.

What little daylight reached the bottom of the pit showed Harry he was sprawled on a flagstone floor. Weeds and spongy moss grew thick between the stones, and they were damp and smelled of raw earth. He pushed himself up to his knees, using his good hand.

The walls were of grey stone, streaked with blackish mildew. In front of him stretched a stone-walled tunnel. After a few yards it was lost in darkness.

Standing, bracing himself against a chill wall, he looked upward. There was no sign of Belphoebe and the mechanical bat in what little of the sky he could see.

"The damn bat works for Orchardson," Harry said to himself. "So what the hell is it doing here?"

And where was it carrying Belphoebe Stowe? To Zaytoon's castle or off to a hideout of Orchardson's?

There were no footholds in the hole he'd unexpectedly

dropped into. Climbing out, even if he had two good hands and all his ribs were in working order, would be damn difficult.

"But if this is an old forgotten passway to the castle, I don't want to get out of here anyway."

He took a last glance at the sky above, then crouched and selected one of the broken old boards from the hatch that had long concealed this hole. Getting out his box of wax matches, Harry struck one with his left hand and set fire to a pile of brush and twigs. He held the end of his three foot scrap of board to the flames. As soon as the board was burning, Harry stamped out the small fire and entered the tunnel.

A thick dampness closed in on him and just beyond the throw of light from his feeble torch he heard the sounds of scurrying.

"Shoo," Harry advised whatever was in his path.

Moving slowly and cautiously along, he started counting off the paces.

By the time he reached fifteen there was darkness in back of him as well as in front.

He was aware of small claws skittering on damp rock, some angry chittering.

Harry kept going, getting the impression he was moving deeper underground as he went ahead.

Fifty paces in.

A hollow dripping off to his left.

A hundred paces.

Something slithered across his foot. He glanced down, but it was gone.

Two hundred.

His makeshift torch sputtered, the flame starting to die.

Harry stopped. Holding the board between his knees, he fished out his matchbox with his left hand. He shook out a match, then transferred it to the fingers that stuck out of the cast and struck the match.

He held it to the burning end of the stick and managed to get the flame to perk up some.

He dropped the box back into his vest pocket and resumed walking.

Three hundred.

Four hundred.

The tunnel, he was near certain, had leveled off.

Six hundred.

Seven hundred.

Eight hundred.

Up ahead Harry saw a stone wall and a heavy oaken door. A large padlock, rusted with age, dangled from it.

"This had better be a way into the damn castle."

Harry thrust the end of his torch into the large upper hinge and it stayed there, giving him a dim, flickering light.

He squatted and tugged at the lock.

It broke apart in his hand. At that same moment the torch died.

Blackness took over the tunnel.

Tiny clawed feet started coming closer across the stones.

He felt for the doorknob. He caught it and turned. Then he pulled at the door. For about a half a minute it didn't budge. Slowly it began to come open. He tugged with his left hand and the available fingers of his right.

Beyond the door stretched a stone corridor. At its end it was joined by two other corridors and in them oil lamps were burning.

Leaving the heavy door open behind him, Harry started toward the light.

Returning to the clouded mirror over his bureau, the Great Lorenzo took another admiring look. "Marvelous," he pronounced. "The entire populace of far Cathay would be fooled."

The magician had tinted his visible skin a pale saffron

hue, pasted on a drooping mandarin moustache and made his eyes look a bit more Oriental.

Pleased, he retreated from the mirror. "But unless Harry and the fair Belphoebe return shortly, I won't be able to do much beyond a slapdash makeup job on the lad." He glanced out a window at the declining day, consulted his pocket watch yet again.

Back at the mirror he gave his disguise another approving inspection.

"Might be worthwhile to use my Shanghai Coffin illusion during this engagement. I could step into the box as myself, reappear downstage an instant later as the Emperor of the Forbidden City of—"

A faint tapping, almost a scratching, sounded on his room door.

The Great Lorenzo trotted across the thin carpet. "Yes?"

There was no response.

Looking down, he noticed that a pale yellow sheet of folded notepaper had been slipped beneath the door.

Puffing, he stooped to pick up the note. "Can it be that the statuesque Senhora Picada has suffered a change of . . . Damn!"

The hand-lettered note read:

> *Mr. Lorenzo: Please inform the authorities that we have Miss B. Stowe. Her life for the obelisk. Details will follow.*
>
> *O.*
>
> *P.S.: We are addressing you rather than Mr. Challenge, since we fear he's dead and gone.*

The room's only armchair groaned when the magician dropped into it.

He read the letter twice again, shaking his head, and

then let the crisp sheet of paper drop to the floor. "Is Harry no more?"

Shutting his eyes, the Great Lorenzo strained to summon up a vision.

The best he could conjure was a strong hunch.

"Harry's alive and at the castle." He stood, hurried to the door. "I've got to journey there right now."

Chapter 16

Harry let himself into another underground room. This one was large and had a vaulted ceiling. It was lit by a row of gas lamps that had been strung along one of the walls. There were weapons everywhere, some set up and ready to demonstrate, the rest in cases and crates.

Making his way slowly through the maze of arms, he spotted cases of repeating rifles, bayonets, sabres and even double-barreled eight-gauge elephant guns. Sitting on a cleared space on the dark stone floor were two wheeled Maxim automatic machine guns, loaded and ready to be fired for prospective customers.

"Zaytoon's pursuit of the obelisk hasn't gotten in the way of his business anyhow."

Harry sat down to rest for a while on a crate of Navy Colts. His ribs were commencing to bother him some. He scanned the room, taking a quick inventory of all the weapons stored there.

"Oh, I say, this is a deuced jolly surprise."

Turning, Harry saw Bertie Pennoyer standing in a doorway across the wide room. "Been hoping I'd run into you."

Pennoyer yanked a .45 revolver from the waistband of his tweed trousers. "One hopes you're not in a foolishly vengeful mood, old boy." He chuckled behind his free hand. "Hurt the old wrist, did we? Pity. Still, could've been worse, eh?"

"I came to get Jennie," he said. "And Professor Stowe."

"That old duffer I'd almost give you gladly, don't you know. Stubborn as a ruddy ox and won't do a blessed thing he's told." Pennoyer came down the three stone steps into the room. "Zaytoon, don't you know, got a bee in his blooming bonnet that he ought to have the sod working for us rather than for that great blubbery Orchardson. Why for pity's sake? I mean to say, who wants a bunch of silly mechanical bats flapping about. Not that the bloke's consented to finish a single one since we've had him nattering about the place."

"How come," asked Harry, not moving from his perch, "you're working for Zaytoon?"

Pennoyer gave another masked chuckle, then rubbed his thumb and forefinger together. "The lucre, old man," he answered. "Pennoyer fortune's been, thanks to my excesses and those of some of my like-minded kinsmen, just about used up. That bloody expedition nearly broke me and the Musée des Antiquités didn't pay anywhere near what they'd promised. Wasn't even able to smuggle much in from Egypt. Nearly on my uppers until recently."

"What's Zaytoon paying you for?"

"I got onto the secret of the obelisk, old man." He leaned casually against the wall, the gaslight making his monocle flash. "Actually, to be perfectly frank, I pilfered old Fodorsky's notes soon as I got wind of what he'd stumbled onto. Fodorsky himself sold the information to that pig Orchardson."

"There really is a secret?"

"Jolly well better be," said Pennoyer. "Turns out the blooming obelisk has a hollowed out section near the tip. Held in that in an ivory casket is a supply of some fabulous lost Egyptian drug that can extend life."

Harry grinned. "You believe that?"

"Inclined to, yes," he said. "Mostly, you know, because old Zaytoon does. Why does he? Because the bloke is actually nine hundred years old. Staggering, what? Nine hundred if he's a day. Means he was born back in . . . um . . . oh, around the year 1000 A.D. Well, when he was still living out his original three score and ten, don't you know, he came across some of this same stuff. Been taking it ever since and he is, as the chaps say, living proof that it works.''

"His original supply is running out?''

"Ran out last week. I'd heard rumors he was scouring the blasted earth for more some months ago,'' said Pennoyer. "So when I was tipped to what old Fodorsky had found and got hold of the info, why, I approached Zaytoon. The rest is history.''

"Why didn't Fodorsky just take the stuff out of the obelisk?''

"Ain't that easy, old man. After he got the heiroglyphs all translated and realized there was a code message hidden in them, he worked that out,'' explained Pennoyer. "That told him that the stuff was in there, but that it was sealed up tight as a drum. Only way to get at it is to saw into the blooming rock with special tools and all that.''

"That's why Zaytoon was trying to scare off the workmen.''

"Exactly. We could've done the job in one night and been off, safe as houses, by dawn.''

Harry stood. "I'd like to see Jennie.''

"Afraid not, old man. Since Jennie Barr knows just as much about the whereabouts of the real obelisk as you do, we don't need you at all,'' said Pennoyer. "You're going to expire right here in the bowels of the—''

"Jennie doesn't know anything about it. But I do.''

Pennoyer hid a chuckle. "Nice try at a bluff, but afraid it won't work. You and she were intimate, don't you know. All you know, she knows.'' He swung the gun until it was pointing directly at Harry.

"This is hardly sporting.''

"What?''

"Okay for Zaytoon to slaughter his opponents,'' Harry

said. "Also acceptable for Orchardson. You, however, are a gentleman."

Pennoyer gasped. "Jove, I do believe you've got something there," he said thoughtfully. "Some things a gentleman simply can't do. Murder in cold bold's one of them."

"So how about a duel?"

"Duel, you say?" He considered. "Yet really, old chap, you're in no shape to—"

"Left hand." Harry held it up. "I say I can beat you with my left hand."

"You're suggesting what—pistols or sabres?"

"Sabres. There's a whole case of them right over there near you."

Pennoyer contemplated the open case. "I feel I must warn you, Challenge, that before I was sent down from Oxford, I excelled in fencing and—"

"Then there's no reason to be afraid."

"Afraid, is it?" He gestured at Harry with his .45. "First, old chap, take your gun out of its holster and drop it safely out of reach."

"Obviously you don't think me a gentleman or you'd trust me not—"

"Very few Americans are gentlemen."

Harry eased out his .38 and tossed it onto the excelsior in an opened case of bayonets. "Just pick out a couple of sabres and toss me one."

Pennoyer rested his own gun on a ledge. "Keep in mind, old chap, that I warned you about my skills in this sport."

"I will."

Pennoyer selected two of the British-style sabres. He gripped each in turn, hefted it, slashed at the air. "Yes, I prefer this one," he decided.

He flung the other three-foot-long blade to Harry.

Harry reached for it with his right hand.

The steel hit his cast, the sabre fell to the stone floor with a clang.

"Damn, forgot my cast." Harry bent to retrieve the sword, but only succeeded in kicking it under one of the standing machine guns.

"I say, if you're that bloody awkward, we can hardly expect a fair contest."

"Hardly." Harry made a sudden dive, got hold of the machine gun, activated it and fired a burst of shots over Pennoyer's surprised head.

"Here now, you—"

"Drop the sabre, Bertie. Raise your hands high."

"Jove, that wasn't at all sporting of you, Challenge."

"We've already established the fact," reminded Harry, "that I'm not a gentleman."

Chapter 17

The day was dying when the man Jennie Barr had never seen before came to fetch her. The shadows in her narrow stone room were deepening and she was lighting the chunky candle on her lame cot-side table.

The heavy door made its usual noises. Standing on the threshold was a thickset man wearing a dark suit and a pale blue turban. His face was pale, his whiskers a washed-out blond. "You will come with me, miss."

She dropped the matchbox to the table. "Odd hour for a firing squad."

"Hurry, please, miss." He held a lantern in his right hand, a .32 revolver of German make in his right. "Should you fail to cooperate en route, I will be obliged to shoot you. Not fatally, yet most painfully."

"Nicest invitation I've had since I checked into this darn hoosegow." She stood, hesitated, then picked up her notebook.

They walked along a twisting corridor, the turbaned man behind her with his gun barrel ready to prod. Up a long chill flight of stone stairs, along another serpentine stone hall, through a vast empty room paneled in dark wood, along a straight corridor, up a flight of hardwood steps, into a hallway that was paneled, carpeted and lit with gas lamps.

"Stop in front of the third door on your left, miss."

Jennie did.

Her guide knocked twice on the thick walnut door, paused, knocked three times again. "You can go in, miss."

"After you."

"I'll be waiting out here, miss."

Shrugging, the reporter opened the door and entered the room beyond.

The coffin was the first thing she saw. It sat on a low platform in front of the large canopied bed. An ebony coffin with fixings of gold. The lid was open.

The only light in the brown bedchamber came from an oil lamp resting on a claw-footed table beside the coffin. Jennie had the impression there was someone in the bed, muffled in the thick shadows.

"Come here, young woman."

Jennie inhaled sharply. "Beg pardon?" She wasn't certain if the thin, dry voice had come from the coffin or the fourposter.

"Here, beside the bed."

As she passed the open coffin, Jennie glanced in. The body of a young dark-haired woman reposed within on a bed of yellowed satin that was streaked with dirt.

There was an old man propped up in the bed. The remains of a man. There seemed to be almost no flesh on his face and Jennie had the impression the multitude of wrinkles were etched directly on the bones of the skull. His head was like some piece of cryptic scrimshaw. Atop the head sat a fezlike cap, crimson with a dark silky tassle. The cap had slipped down to almost the brow ridges of the nearly fleshless skull. The man's neck was as thin as an axe handle and it rose out of the stained collar of the silk smoking jacket he wore. Under the jacket he had on a suit of faded long underwear and the topmost buttons showed. Both his hands were outside the tufted covers, folded over his sunken midsection. The wrists were sticks, the hands themselves looked brittle and mummified.

"I am Anwar Zaytoon," he gasped in his dusty voice. "I discovered the secret of life eternal."

Jennie coughed into her hand. "I'm too polite to make the obvious rejoinder."

A strange, awful sound began rattling and wheezing around in his narrow chest. "You manage," he said, when he was finished laughing, "to be droll even when in danger, Miss Barr. Yes, I am full aware I look more like death than life."

"This secret you found, what does it have to do with the obelisk?"

Zaytoon didn't reply for a moment. "In Damascus in the year 986 A.D.," he began at last, "I discovered a supply of a rare drug developed many centuries earlier in my native Egypt. It was derived from the now extinct tana plant. This supply was sufficient to keep me alive, when administered in conjunction with certain mystical rituals, until this day."

"You're over nine hundred years old?" Her fingers tapped at the notebook she was clutching. "How does that feel? What are your reactions to the—"

"This is not the time for an interview, young woman," he cut in. "My supply of the tana drug has, at long last, run out."

"Haven't you been scouting before this?"

"Always, obviously," Zaytoon answered in his dim faraway voice. "In Tyre in the thirteenth century I found a small amount that had somehow been preserved, unbeknownst to its owners over the centuries, in a funerary urn. Another small quantity I was able to add to my store in the seventeenth century. It had been mistakenly stored with some Christian relics in a country church in Livonia."

"You killed people to get it?"

"When necessary."

"And the obelisk will tell you how to get more?"

"It contains more. There is nearly a pound concealed in a hollowed compartment inside the Osiris Obelisk."

"Did you find that out from Professor Fodorsky?"

"Only indirectly, since he chose to sell his knowledge to a rival of mine named Max Orchardson," said Zaytoon, his thin lips curling. "That man has committed more sins in one lifetime than I have in centuries."

Jennie asked, "A pound is good for how many more years?"

"At least five hundred," answered the old man. "In that time, given the impressive strides being made in the realm of science, I have no doubt that we shall be able to find a way to manufacture the tana drug synthetically."

"Then you could live for ever and ever."

"Such is my intention," he replied. "The terror of death felt by an ordinary mortal is, I assure you, nothing when compared to those fears that plague me. The longer you live, the less inclined you are to—"

"You'd really want to live hundreds of years more in the shape you're in now?"

"Ah, but the tana drug also rejuvenates as well," he told her. "Once I begin taking it again, I'll soon assume the appearance of a relatively young man of fifty or sixty."

"Well, more power to you I guess," said Jennie. "Thing is, I can't help you at all. Since I have no idea where—"

"Don't tire yourself, Anwar. Let me question this stubborn young woman."

Jennie looked toward the coffin. The dark-haired young woman was sitting up now, smiling at her.

It took Harry just under five minutes to pick the lock of Jennie's cell. If his right hand hadn't been in a cast he could've done it in two.

He straightened, pulled the door slowly open.

The stone room was empty.

"Damn, did Bertie give me a bum steer?"

He had the impression that Pennoyer, now trussed, gagged and stored among the weapons, told him the truth about where Jennie Barr was being held.

Glancing around the candlelit room, Harry noticed the stub of a pencil beside the flickering candle. "She was here."

After shutting the cell door, he stood in the grey corridor for a moment.

"Old Zaytoon ought to know where Jennie is."

And Pennoyer had also told him where to find the arms merchant.

Harry, somewhat awkwardly, reached inside his coat and managed to draw out his .38 revolver. He tucked it into his belt and started along the corridor.

Several hundred twisting yards later he came to the steep flight of stone steps Pennoyer had told him about. Harry climbed these and then hurried quietly along another snaking corridor.

He carefully opened the wooden door at the hall end. An enormous room lay beyond, its walls paneled in dark wood, its high ceiling crossed with thick beams. In the dust on the black and white floor he made out the recent footprints of a woman and a man.

The hall leading away from the room was hung with faded tapestries across which courtly knights and fair maidens rode in eternal pilgrimage. He went up another flight of stairs and found himself standing in an arched doorway.

Midway down the gaslit hall a broad man wearing a turban was leaning beside a door. His back was, thus far, turned to Harry.

Harry tiptoed along the carpeting. When he was about three feet behind the turbaned guard, he reached out and tapped him on the shoulder.

The stocky man flinched, started to spin around.

Harry hit him in the temple with the butt of his gun, holding the weapon in his left hand. Because of the guard's tuban and because Harry didn't have as much strength in his left as in his right hand, it took three whaps with the gun to knock the man out.

Harry caught him, dragged him along to a nearby alcove

and dumped him in there. Using the turban, he gagged and tied him. He appropriated the guard's .45, stuffing it into his pocket.

"Spoils the look of my suit."

He returned to the door, opened it and walked in, grinning amiably.

"Harry," said Jennie happily. She was seated in a wing chair that had been pulled over beside the fourposter bed.

Naida Strand, wearing a floor-length velvet gown, was standing over her. The expression on her face mingled recognition, amusement and scorn.

The old man on the bed croaked, "Who is this audacious young man? What does he mean by—"

"This is my dear old friend Harry Challenge," said Naida, toying with the ruby brooch around her pale neck.

"Challenge? Pennoyer killed him, days ago."

"Apparently not," said Naida.

Harry took his revolver out and gestured at the dark-haired woman. "Jennie'll be leaving now."

Jennie stood, notebook pressed to her breasts. "Yes, I will," she seconded. "Thanks for having me."

Naida's smile was thin and cold. "You forget, dear Harry, that your gun can't harm me," she reminded. "Surely, after all your experience in matters occult, you know a vampire can't be killed with ordinary bullets."

He grinned again. "Yep, I know that, ma'am," he answered. "Which is why I have six silver bullets loaded in here. Had them cast while I was laid up in the hospital in Kaltzonburg. Took a fall off a train a few days back."

Jennie moved around the bed, walked by the coffin and came to Harry's side. "I'm glad you survived."

"I was sort of pleased myself."

"He's bluffing you, Naida," said Zaytoon. "Take the gun out of my bedside table and kill him."

She was studying Harry's face, still standing straight beside the chair. "I'm inclined to agree," Naida said. "Until you walked into this bedchamber, Harry, you didn't even know I was in partnership with Anwar Zaytoon. Therefore, you couldn't have prepared silver—''

"You put a lot more faith in Bertie Pennoyer than he deserves," said Harry. "He didn't kill me as instructed and he talked quite a lot about you folks before he escorted me off that damn train. Talked about Zaytoon, about the secret of the obelisk and about you, Nadia.''

"You're bluffing, just as Anwar—''

"I let you live before." His voice was harsh now. "That was a mistake. This time I won't be sentimental.''

She took a step back toward the table. "No, I don't believe you."

He raised the gun, aimed it directly at her. "Well, if this was a poker game, about now'd be the time to call,'' Harry said. "You go for that gun, Naida, and I shoot you. With real silver bullets. The kind no vampire can—''

"Damn you." She turned, ran suddenly for a window. Tugging it open, she dived out into the darkness.

"Bluff worked," he said.

Jennie said, "Harry, she committed—''

"Nope, there are balconies along this side of the castle. I spotted them when I was casing the place this afternoon,'' he said. "Naida's probably scrambling down the side of the tower now. Let's go, since I want to get you out of—''

"You'll go nowhere," cried Zaytoon. He was fighting with his covers, gnarled hands clawing at them. "I'll stop you myself.''

The old man managed to throw the covers aside. With an enormous effort he rolled to the bed edge and thrust his stick-thin legs out and to the floor. He stepped free of the bed and stood up.

There was a brittle cracking sound, and another. Both legs snapped and the bones came poking through the yellow parchment skin.

Zaytoon gasped with pain but made an attempt to get to the table for the gun. Instead he fell to the carpet.

More cracking, splintering sounds. His ancient body was crumbling, breaking up.

"My god, Harry," whispered Jennie.

"C'mon." He took her arm. "We still have to get Professor Stowe out of here."

Zaytoon was a tumble of twisted clothes and splintered bones. The nightcap had fallen free and lay next to the chair leg, the tassle was powdered with the scaly dust that had been the old man's skin.

"He was nine hundred years old," said Jennie as Harry hurried her across the room.

"Should've picked up a little wisdom in all that time." He opened the door.

Chapter 18

Professor G.P.R. Stowe said, "That is typical of my daughter, all too typical." He was a short, rumpled man with frizzled grey hair. "Arranges to have me rescued, do you see, and neglects to send sufficient hands to take care of all my luggage."

"We don't have time for baggage," explained Harry. "Zaytoon is dead, but there's still a castle filled with toadies and thugs who don't know that."

They were standing in the middle of the professor's combination bedroom and workshop. Stowe was swaying some, a cut-glass decanter of rum in his hand. Stretched out on the unmade bed was a nearly completed flying bat.

"Someone will come back for your stuff later," promised Jennie.

"I notice, more in sadness than in anger, that Belphoebe did not even see her way clear to—"

"She was carried off by one of your damn bats."

"Why ever did she let that happen to her?"

"It was more Orchardson's idea," said Harry. "I made sure, in a recent conversation with Bertie Pennoyer, that Zaytoon doesn't have any of your gadgets in operation yet."

"How can he, when the first is lying yonder upon—"

"We'll go now," said Harry.

"Young man, you do not seem to comprehend—and

considering you are a gentleman friend of my daughter your denseness is accounted for—you do not understand my position. I am tired of being kidnapped by all and sundry and each time losing more and more of my personal and business—"

"There are two ways you can leave here," Harry cut in. "Willingly or unconscious."

The professor blinked, took a swig of rum, wiped his mouth on his lab coat sleeve and frowned. "Are you threatening me, young man?"

Harry grinned. "You're damn right."

"See here, I . . . um . . . very well." He'd noticed Harry's left hand turning into a fist. "I, I assure you, Belphoebe is in for a severe dressing-down."

"We have to get her back from Orchardson before you can do that," said Harry.

Harry, Jennie and the stumbling, muttering Professor Stowe were coming down a splendid carved wooden staircase and were only a few hundred feet from the main door out of the castle when three large, swarthy men in evening clothes entered the immense hall below.

They noted the strangers on the stairway and proceeded to draw revolvers and a dagger.

"Far be it from me to criticize, young man," said the frizzle-haired professor, "but attempting to exit by the most obvious— "

"Been lucky bluffing so far," said Harry. "I thought we could work it once more."

"Maybe we can," said Jennie.

Harry stepped ahead of the other two. "You men down there," he called. "Hurry, run to the kitchen and start boiling plenty of hot water."

"Gar?" The biggest of the three men was crouched at the foot of the stairs with his revolver in his fist.

"I'm Herr Doctor Hauser," Harry explained, "and I

have just come from Herr Zaytoon's chambers. I fear he's had a serious relapse and must be—''

"Kill the infidels!" shouted another of the guards, the one with the knife.

"Death to intruders! By the Eye of Osiris!"

The three large men started up the stairs, howling, waving their assorted lethal weapons.

"You convinced *me* you were a medic," said Jennie.

"Duck behind me." He reached for his gun.

"Halt, you craven dogs!" boomed another voice down below, "lest the wrath of Isis vist you."

"Gar?" The guards halted, still fifty feet from Harry and Jennie.

A plump Oriental gentleman had appeared out of a dining room off the hallway. He held his silken-sleeved arms high. "I must request that you cease this unseemly display of mean-minded behavior at once," he informed the perplexed guards. "For not only am I a guest at tonight's buffet supper, I am a most powerful Eastern wizard."

"Kill him, too," suggested the guard with the knife.

The Great Lorenzo sighed, his Oriental moustache drooping even further. "You gents give me no choice," he said. "Lando Zambini Marvelo!"

From out of nowhere great sputtering clouds of thick green smoke began to billow. They came rolling up the stairs to engulf everyone. Blood-chilling shrieks were heard, strange ominous shapes danced in the dense green swirls.

"Get down here fast, my boy!"

Harry caught Jennie's arm and the professor's. "Let's go," he said. "Keep over to the far left."

"This latest nonsense," muttered the professor, "is almost more than I can stand."

Chapter 19

The main square in Kaltzonburg was filled with morning mist. The Great Lorenzo slackened his pace and then stopped in front of a frail old woman who was vending violets. "A moment, Harry," he said. "Be so kind as to give me a bunch of your very best blossoms, dear lady." He pulled a gold coin from behind his ear, handing it to her.

"Why, you must be the Great Lorenzo." She accepted the money and gave him the flowers.

"Ah, little mother, you've seen and enjoyed my magical extravaganza?"

"I fear I can't afford it, sir. But I saw your portrait, which hardly does you justice, in the newspaper only yesterday."

He upended the bunch of violets, shook them. Two tickets fell into his palm. "Here are a couple of free passes."

"God bless you, sir."

Taking hold of Harry's arm, the magician resumed their walk. "I never get over the gratification that fame brings."

"Did I notice greasepaint on that sweet old grandmother's face?"

"She is not a shill, my boy."

"Good, because I'm already impressed by your many abilities. No need to hire a—"

"Here I brighten the poor old wretch's otherwise drab existence by giving her a choice pair of seats in the second balcony and you suggest that—"

"There's Inspector Swann."

The French policeman was seated at a bench and facing one of the tables set out for chess and checker players. "Good morning, monsieurs," he said. "Thanks to your communication of last evening, Harry, I was able to alert the Kaltzonburg police and we raided Zaytoon's castle."

"What about Jean-Pierre Pastoral and the rest of your men who were on the train?" Harry seated himself on the opponent bench.

"All alive and being kept prisoner in the castle."

"We didn't have time, or the forces, to rescue them all last night."

"One quite understands." Reaching into his breast pocket, he brought out several sheets of folded paper. "First I . . . Ah, very impressive, M. Lorenzo."

"Hum? Oh, the stogie." The magician, leaning against the back of Harry's bench, had picked a lighted cigar out of his handful of violets. "Care for a smoke?"

"Not at the moment." Swann spread a page of pale grey paper out on the inlaid checkerboard. "This Bertie Pennoyer we found exactly where you told us he would be. He is being held on a number of charges, including kidnapping and train hijacking. Of Mlle. Naida Strand there was no trace. Nor did we find the remains of Anwar Zaytoon."

Harry said, "What was left of him was right beside the bed. In the same room with the damn coffin."

Shaking his head, Inspector Swann said, "We found no coffin either."

"The dark lady returned after we took our leave," suggested the Great Lorenzo, "to do a bit of tidying up."

"Sooner or later I'm going to catch her," said Harry.

Swann unfolded another sheet. "Here is the latest communication from Orchardson," he said. "In your absence,

M. Lorenzo, I took the liberty of intercepting this. It arrived last evening while you were otherwise occupied at the castle.''

"What's he want?" asked Harry.

Swann handed him the sheet of pale green notepaper. "See for yourself."

The note read:

> *The obelisk is to be delivered to the red hunting lodge on the north shore of Lake Langweilig at 4:00 P.M. this Friday. Miss Stowe will be turned over to you at that time. No tricks, if you please.*

> O.

"This particular lake," said Harry, "is about thirty miles south of here. As I recall from my map studying of the other day."

"Twenty-seven miles, yes," said Swann.

"Okay, so we have three days to get everything ready."

"What do you have in mind?"

"First, we have to open up the obelisk," said Harry.

"The baron will never allow such a valuable—"

"When he hears what's inside, he will," Harry assured him. "Almost everybody's interested in immortality."

"Eh? Do you mean such an awesome secret as—"

"That's what's inside the obelisk, yep."

"Even so, how are we to gain access to—"

"I've already arranged for that," said the Great Lorenzo, puffing on his cigar. "Thanks to kindhearted Prince Rudy, and a few of my own local connections, I have both a crackerjack safe blower and a gifted stonemason standing by. The latter fellow specialized in mournful angels for high-class tombs, but he can saw through stone like—"

"We also have to put Professor Stowe to work on a device he was explaining to me on our ride back from Lowen last night," said Harry.

"Another flying machine, monsieur?"

"Nope, something that can control the ones that already exist," answered Harry.

". . . then there was the redhead who was the understudy for the part of Little Eva in a traveling company of a German version of *Uncle Tom's Cabin*," Jennie was explaining. "He settled with her for $25,000. Next came an American girl named, so help me, Pansy Dorf. She was a sharpshooter with a rundown wild West show fronted by Colonel Buckskin Dan. Her attorneys claimed—"

"To sum up all your digging into the baron's background," interrupted Harry, "the guy is fond of women."

"Fond may not be a strong enough word." She glanced up from her notebook. "Do you want to hear about the tattooed Swedish girl known as the Portable Museum?"

"Nope," decided Harry.

They were on the wide terrace of Baron Felix Groll's château in the wooded hills above Kaltzonburg. The morning mist had gone but the midday sunlight was thin and pale.

Jennie closed her notebook. "In residence at the moment is a lady calling herself Lulu Cortez," she said. "She was stranded in Urbania four months ago when the touring Graustark National Ballet Company went bankrupt."

"How old is she?"

"Twenty-two."

"And the baron is . . . what? . . . fifty-five?"

"Claims fifty-five. Actually, he's fifty-nine."

Harry nodded. "He's about to join us."

One of the French doors facing the terrace opened and a slender man in a blue blazer and grey trousers came walking toward them. His short-cropped hair and beard were grey. "Ah, it is Herr Challenge and Fraulein Barr," he said, bowing, smiling, clicking his heels. "Much have I heard of both of you." Taking hold of Jennie's hand, he bent and kissed it. "Your series on the tenements of New

York City brought tears to my eyes. Ah, and your articles on the recent unpleasantness at Blackwood Castle caused my hackles to rise as I perused it, my dear.''

"Why, thank you.''

Harry said, "We didn't mean to get you out of your sickbed, baron. But since we're working against time, I—''

"Sick? Who is sick? I have been up for hours attending to my business affairs.''

Harry grinned. "Excuse me. It's only that you seem . . . Well, I guess for a man of sixty you don't look all that bad.''

"Sixty? I am but fifty-four.'' He frowned at Harry, then returned his attention to Jennie. "You are one of the most perceptive and objective reporters in the world, fraulein. I put it to you, do I appear to be sixty years of age?''

"No, I wouldn't peg you at anything beyond fifty-nine.''

Baron Groll paused to breathe in and out. "I must inform you, Herr Challenge, that you are not putting me in a receptive mood to grant any favors,'' he told Harry. "I am informed you wish to make a—''

"You'll have to forgive us,'' said Harry. "It's just that I've got this rejuvenation drug on my mind. Naturally, I'm going to be doubly aware of the sad effects of aging on a once handsome and vital—''

"Rejuvenation?'' said the baron. "I was told some lunatic wanted my lovely new obelisk in exchange for a young woman. By the way, she is beautiful?''

Jennie began. "Plain as a—''

"Belphoebe Stowe is quite a handsome woman,'' said Harry, nudging Jennie. "And she'd be eternally grateful to any man who—''

"Might we return to this talk of rejuvenation?''

Harry rested his backside against the marble railing that guarded the terrace. "I'm going to confide an enormously important secret in you, baron,'' he said. "Inside your obelisk, hidden for centuries, is a supply of tana.''

"Of what?"

"It's a powerful drug," explained the reporter. "Anwar Zaytoon used the stuff and he lived to be nine hundred."

"Nine hundred? But that's imposs—"

"And up until the very end he didn't look a day over sixty."

"Fifty," suggested Harry.

"Fifty," amended Jennie. "That's right. Zaytoon was nine hundred, yet he appeared to be younger than you."

The baron stroked his beard, gazing thoughtfully out at the green woodlands surrounding his château. "You are certain this drug is concealed in my obelisk?"

"It is," Harry assured him. "As the owner of the obelisk, anything inside it is yours."

"I could look even younger," he inquired, "and never die?"

"That's the idea," said Jennie. "Harry knows exactly where the stuff is and how to get it out without damaging the obelisk much at all."

"Can have my crew here within the hour," Harry said.

Baron Groll asked, "What do you want in return?"

"The loan of the obelisk."

"Loan? As I understand it this decadent mystic wants it for good and all."

"We'll take the obelisk apart, extract the cache of tana, put it back together and borrow it for about a day."

"Merely borrow?"

"Harry has a way figured out to prevent Orchardson from keeping the thing."

"Then I will have this miraculous drug and my obelisk?"

"That's right."

"Very well, you have my permission to do what must be done," the baron said. "Ah, but you must not mention any of this to my friend, Lulu Cortez. I want to surprise her."

"Not a word," promised Harry.

Chapter 20

The Great Lorenzo rotated his hand in the twilight. His gold watch climbed free of his waistcoat pocket, floated up to his hand. "I must be off, children," he announced. "Curtain time in two hours."

Harry and Jennie were again on the terrace of Baron Groll's château.

"The crew you provided ought to have the damn obelisk uncorked any time now," said Harry. "Why not stay and—"

"It is my motto, my boy, never to keep my eager public waiting." The magician manually returned his watch to his pocket. "Besides I have a feeling . . . Ah, but no need to play the wet blanket. Farewell until the morrow."

"Whoa now," said Harry.

"You're not going to leave," said Jennie, "without giving us the benefit of your latest magical insight."

" 'Tis not a vision," he told them, "merely a hunch."

"And?" asked Harry.

"You—or rather the anxious baron is in for a bit of a disappointment perhaps." The Great Lorenzo adjusted his top hat, adjusted his cloak and went striding off across the terrace and down the marble staircase that led to the front drive where his carriage waited.

"What's he hinting at?" Jennie watched the magician disappear into the gathering dusk.

"That maybe there's nothing inside the obelisk."

"But there has to be. All these people couldn't be chasing after nothing."

"Wouldn't be the first time." He walked over and sat on the marble railing.

She perched beside him. "We ought to be back inside. Thing should be just about open."

"Inspector Swann'll holler," said Harry. "Unless you feel your readers could use a few more details on granite sawing and—"

"Darn it, Harry." She punched his arm. "Just lay off me, okay?"

"I didn't mean to—"

"We're both pretty enthusiastic about our jobs," she said. "You wouldn't drop a case you were investigating to come off with me. So don't razz me when I—"

"Sure I would. Where do you want me to come off to?"

She turned to study his profile. "Paris wasn't so bad. Let's go back there."

"When?"

Jennie sighed. "There's the same darn snag," she said. "You won't leave Urbania until Belphoebe Stowe's safe. I won't pack up until I file my story on the rescue."

"We'll both be finished by Friday," he said. "By Monday we can be back in Paris."

"The *Daily Inquirer* owes me a week of vacation," she said. "At least."

"Okay, then we'll spend a week in Paris. But without giant bats or—"

"Walking mummies or—"

"Aggressive Zouaves." Harry put his good arm around her waist, leaned and kissed her.

"Ahum," came the voice of Inspector Swann from an open French door. "They are ready to open it." He went away.

"And no obelisks," said Jennie.

*   *   *

The stonemason was a small, dark man in smock and work trousers. Covered with granite dust, he was crouched at the tip of the lying-down obelisk. A makeshift scaffolding was supporting the apex.

"Easy now, chum," advised the dapper safecracker. A tall, lean man, he was standing close by with a stethoscope dangling from his left hand.

"We are ready," said the mason.

The safecracker dropped the stethoscope into his coat pocket, took hold of the tip of the obelisk. The mason did likewise.

Baron Groll was pacing along the canvas that had been spread out on the floor of his conservatory. "Get on with it," he urged.

"Lend a hand," Inspector Swann told the two uniformed Kaltzonburg policemen who'd been standing watch.

Grunting and puffing, the four men lifted the apex free of the obelisk and let it rest on the scaffolding.

"The mason mentioned earlier," said Swann to Harry, "there is evidence that's been taken off before and very artfully replaced."

"Sure, they did that back in ancient Egypt when the—"

"More recently than that, monsieur."

Jennie tapped Harry's arm. "Lorenzo's hunch," she said quietly.

The safecracker was on his knees, shining a bull's-eye lantern into the opening that was now visible. There was a hollowed out cube about the size of a shoebox. "Got to be mighty careful," he said. "On the lookout for poisoned needles and other such engines of destruction."

"There's a small ivory casket in there," said the baron. "Get it out, will you?"

"All in good time." The safecracker rubbed his fingertips on his palms.

"Ah, I have no more patience." Barol Groll pushed him aside and thrust in his hand. He pulled out a casket of gold-trimmed ivory. "Is this it, Herr Challenge?"

"Ought to be."

"Foolish," muttered the safecracker. "Don't know what sort of trap them old Gypsies set."

The baron, hands shaking some, put the casket on a marble-topped table. He took hold of the lid.

"Could also be," said the safecracker, "they rigged a spring device in the lid to shoot a—"

"There, I've open . . ." Baron Groll stared into the open casket. "There is nothing . . . only this folded piece of paper."

Harry had moved to the table. He lifted the page from the box and unfolded it. "Well, now."

"Harry," said Jennie, "what is it?"

"I'll read it to everybody," he said. " 'To whom it may concern: Should anyone else ever solve the cipher, I offer my sympathies. I have already taken the tana drug but left the casket and this note. The work was done in the hold of the ship bringing this ugly artifact back from Egypt to Paris. My colleagues, a simpleminded lot, know nothing of this. Quite frankly, I don't believe anyone else will ever be clever enough to find out, as I have, the secret of the obelisk of Osiris. Yet my vanity prompts me to write this down and take claim for solving a riddle that eluded all others for thousands of years. The drug is mine and I am now assured of living forever. Most sincerely yours, Sir Munson Bellhouse.' " Harry let the note drop to the tabletop.

"Orchardson killed Bellhouse," said Jennie.

"To keep him from learning the secret of the obelisk," said Harry.

"The current whereabouts of the tana drug," said Jennie. "Only Bellhouse knew that and he's dead now."

Baron Groll glanced from Harry to Jennie and back to Harry again. "I can't follow all this," he said, "yet I have the uneasy impression I'm not going to live forever or even be rejuvenated."

"That about," said Harry, "sums it up."

Chapter 21

Friday was grey and misty. When they reached Lake Langweilig, a light rain began to fall.

The Great Lorenzo had been expecting rain and was wearing a yellow slicker and matching hat. He and Harry were sharing the driver's seat of the lumbering circus wagon the obelisk was being hauled in. "Is that our destination I espy across the placid waters, my boy?" He flicked the reins of the four sturdy draft horses who were pulling the wagon.

Harry lowered his binoculars. "Only red hunting lodge in sight."

"Red's a handsome color."

"For circus wagons."

"I rather like this vehicle. Its crimson exterior and gilded bars add a nice touch of brightness to a drab day," said the magician. "And the words enscribed above the cage—*The Wildman of Sulu*—are rather fetching. All in all, I'm delighted I borrowed it from some of my old circus cronies."

Harry was studying the lodge, which was still two miles away, through the glasses again. "Looks like somebody's inside the place," he said. "And . . . yep . . . I'm near certain there's at least one of Stowe's flying machines roosting in those trees beyond the lodge."

"Then your scheme ought to work," the magician said. "If you can keep the professor sober back there."

A coach, with Inspector Swann at the reins and Jennie and Professor Stowe inside, was following behind them.

"Jennie'll see to that."

"An admirable young woman, my boy," he said. "Were I you, I'd settle down with her in a little bower by the side of the road in some quaint small town in the hinterland of America and there—"

"She's not the settling down kind."

"Ah, but love can work—"

"Nor am I." Harry lowered the binoculars.

"Do both of you intend to keep galavanting around the world until you're as long in the tooth as the late Zaytoon?"

"We'll keep on about like this for a while, bumping into each other now and then."

The Great Lorenzo sighed. "Let us turn, before my tender heart breaks, to more mundane topics," he suggested. "Is that gadget of Stowe's really going to do the trick?"

"He assures me it will."

"The professor, brilliant fellow though he is, fails to inspire my full and unqualified confidence," said the magician. "Possibly that impression was created when I found him flat on his back and snoring on the floor of the temporary laboratory you fixed up for him at the baron's."

"He's got a fondness for the bottle."

"So I concluded when the fumes from his sprawled carcass made me tipsy."

Harry said, "There's really no way to test that control panel he built for us. He claims he can use it to take over control of the flying machines from Orchardson. If he can, then that'll be the easiest way to nab Orchardson."

"And even if not, we'll still be able to exchange this dornick for the fair Belphoebe."

Harry nodded. "I want Orchardson, too," he said. "Any hunches?"

Shrugging, the Great Lorenzo replied, "Nary a one. We'll simply have to trust to chance."

The crimson steps of the hunting lodge creaked as Max Orchardson came down them. He wore a tweed suit and hiking boots. "Look around you, Challenge," he advised.

"Already have." Harry had climbed down from the circus wagon and was standing near the edge of the misty lake.

The Great Lorenzo was at the rear of the wagon, unlocking the cage that held the obelisk.

"Three of my men, all armed, are out there in the woods," Orchardson came thumping toward Harry. "As well as two of my highly dependable aerodromes."

"I noticed."

"There are, in addition, three armed men inside the lodge," added the immense, pale Orchardson. "One, armed with a shotgun, stands guard over Miss Stowe in the room directly above the entryway."

"We didn't come to make trouble or get into a brawl," Harry assured him. "You take the obelisk, we take Belphoebe Stowe."

"And you're welcome to her." Orchardson started waddling toward the rear of the circus wagon. "I thought her wretched father was the most quarrelsome person on the face of the planet, until I took this young lady under my roof."

"That's one of the drawbacks of kidnapping: you don't know how your victims are going to behave."

"Not a bad remark, Challenge. I may be able to fashion it into an epigram." Stopping at the open cage, he squinted at the obelisk. "Appears to be authentic." From a coat pocket he took a magnifying glass. First he tapped the granite base with the handle, then he scrutinized it with the lens. "I hear tell, by the by, that Anwar Zaytoon has fallen on hard times."

"He's dead."

"Delightful." He continued to inspect the obelisk. "Were you responsible for his shuffling off?"

"Indirectly," said Harry. "The official cause of death was old age."

"Yes, one can see where it would be." Orchardson slipped the glass into a tweedy pocket, took two rocking steps back. "I am satisfied, Challenge. If you and your fat friend will now retreat to the vicinity of your coach, I'll give the signal for Miss Stowe to be released."

"Fine. Pleasure doing business with you."

He and the Great Lorenzo started walking toward the coach, which was parked several hundred yards down the shore of the lake.

All at once leaves rattled on their left.

From out of the woods a giant mechanical bat came flapping.

"Watch out." Harry shoved the magician down, dived to the pebbly ground himself.

The bat ignored them and sailed over. It hovered above Orchardson for an instant, then grabbed him up.

"Fools, what are you doing?" cried the fat man.

The bat rose up, carrying the thrashing, struggling Orchardson in its clawed arms.

It rose higher and higher and went flying out over the lake.

Crouched, Harry watched. "Damn, Stowe moved too soon."

"Demon rum has dulled his perceptions perhaps."

When the flying machine was four hundred feet above the waters of the lake, it opened its claws.

Orchardson plummeted, screaming, down through the afternoon. He hit the water with an enormous slamming splash and sank at once.

Chapter 22

Harry tugged, left-handed, his revolver out of his belt. "Give me a diversion, Lorenzo."

Yanking off his yellow slicker hat, Lorenzo started hopping on the beach. "El Carim Zanzibar Zatara!"

Purple smoke commenced pouring from the hat, great thick clouds of it. The smoke engulfed the circus wagon, covered a long stretch of the lakeshore and surrounded the lodge. It hid Harry from the gunmen in the woods and from those still inside.

"Excuse my using the same trick twice," called the magician.

Harry went sprinting for the house, revolver in his left hand. He could barely make out the steps, but he went charging up them and shoved on into the lodge.

Just inside the front door he collided with a large coughing man. The man was heavyset, puzzled and carried a .45 revolver absently in his hand.

"The whole place is on fire," warned Harry. "Get all the women and children out fast."

"To be sure, sir . . . what children?"

Smoke came spilling into the rustic living room, blurring everything.

Harry dodged the distracted guard, ran up the wooden staircase to the second floor.

Purplish smoke was forcing itself in through the open windows and the hall was clouded with it.

"Fire!" yelled Harry. "Fire and pestilence!"

"How's that again?" A bald-headed man, cradling a shotgun, stepped out of the room where Belphoebe Stowe was being held.

"This whole lodge is going to blow sky high," explained Harry. "Get out while you can."

"A moment, sir. I recognize you as Harry Challenge, a fellow who's opposed to our . . . oof!"

Harry hit him hard in the midsection with his cast. He punched him twice more in the temple and stepped clear as he slumped to the hardwood floor and was covered by billowing smoke.

"Belphoebe?"

"Mr. Challenge." The blonde young woman appeared in the doorway. "Whatever is going on?"

"Essentially, this is a rescue." He took hold of her arm. "Your nitwit father seems to have murdered Orchardson and that's meant a bit of improvising."

"What is the cause of all this dreadful smoke?"

"Lorenzo. He had some left over from a stunt he pulled the other night," he answered, heading her toward the back stairs. "C'mon. Run."

"I truly appreciate your efforts on my behalf."

They hit the stairs and went rushing down.

Harry was reaching for the back door handle when a third guard stepped out of the purple smoke and pointed a pistol at them. "Be so kind as to stop."

"Oh, nonsense." Belphoebe, who was three steps from the bottom, leaped through the cloudy air and executed a perfect tackle.

The nonplussed guard fell over backwards, fired a shot into an elk head mounted on the wall.

Harry jumped, stepped on his wrist. The gun went spinning from the man's grasp.

Stepping over him after grabbing up the gun, Belphoebe

followed Harry out of the lodge and into even denser smoke.

The Great Lorenzo called to Harry, "How many guards did he mention were lurking amidst the flora?"

"Three." Harry aimed his reply at the spot he assumed the magician was standing.

"I thought as much," the Great Lorenzo said, walking closer and materializing out of the smoke. "In that case, I've succeeded in rendering the lot of them unconscious with a blackjack once presented to me by a fellow who claimed to be a former member of the Gashouse Gang."

As the smoke began to lift, Jennie came running along the beach to Harry. "You're alive," she said, smiling and hugging him.

"I am," he agreed, kissing her.

Inspector Swann, gun in hand, headed for the lodge. "I shall take care of any loose ends within," he said. "You two, let me add, displayed much inventiveness this day."

Belphoebe was watching Harry and the red-haired reporter. "This bears out all I have heard about the behavior of Americans."

"No one would consider you unladylike, Miss Stowe," said the Great Lorenzo, "should you demonstrate your gratitude to your rescuers in some physical way."

"Yes, I believe I shall." She marched over to the magician, kissed him, briefly, on his cheek. "My heartiest thanks."

He put his yellow rain hat back on, tugging it down. "I'm deeply touched," he informed her. "Harry, my boy, we'd best hog-tie the Orchardson forces scattered in the woods and then collect them into our barred wagon."

"Soon as I ask the professor why in the hell he—"

"Revenge," said Jennie. "That's what he told me while I was trying to struggle with him and get him to put Orchardson down gently on dry land."

"Our original plan was to pluck him up with one of his

flying bats after Belphoebe was free and before he could start off with the damn obelisk."

"He claims the sight of Orchardson brought back all he's suffered at his hands," said Jennie, nose wrinkling.

"It sounds as though my deplorable parent has caused yet another—"

"Belphoebe, my beloved child!" The door of the coach came flapping open. Stowe tumbled out, hit the beach with a sloppy thud.

"There are times when I truly wish my loyalty to that awful man was not so strong."

"Help me up, will you? I seem to have developed a cramp from sitting so long in this drafty conveyance." Stowe got to his knees, rubbing at his thigh.

Belphoebe took a few unenthusiastic steps in his direction. "Mr. Challenge informs me that you came very close, father, you wicked old man, to undermining the entire plan."

"Can you blame a father for revenging himself upon the very man who defiled his firstborn jewel and—"

"Orchardson was not at all interested in women, as you well know. Even if he had been, I could easily have eluded the advances of one so grossly over—"

"Yes, yes, go ahead. Scorn and malign me for risking life and limb to save you from a fate worse than—"

"Father, I suggest you climb back inside that coach at once and cease your unseemly behavior."

The professor was upright, more or less, at last. He brushed dirt from his wrinkled suit. "The ingratitude you're displaying, dearest, is more unseemly than—"

"Did you mention, Mr. Lorenzo, that you are in need of assistance in tying up some of those dreadful, debased brutes who have been my captors?"

"All help is most gratefully accepted," he told her. "Come along into yon forest glade with me."

Professor Stowe jerked a wad of handkerchief out and commenced sobbing into it.

"Would you mind, Harry," asked Jennie, "if I rode back on the wagon with you?"

Chapter 23

The Great Lorenzo tipped his top hat and six milk-white doves came fluttering out.

The enthusiastic audience in the packed Spielzeug Theater applauded.

"Tonight, ladies and gentlemen, I am pleased to introduce yet another brand-new and never before seen illusion," he announced, winking in the direction of the box occupied by Harry and Jennie. "Or is it an illusion? Can a man, a mere mortal, actually walk through solid stone? Attend well, for you are about to witness what I call the Curse of the Obelisk illusion."

The houselights dimmed, the gilded curtains behind him slowly parted.

"Not a bad replica," said Jennie, nodding at the pinkish obelisk that stood in the spotlight, flanked by two handsome young women in diaphanous and vaguely Egyptian gowns.

"Obelisks aren't my idea of entertainment," said Harry.

"Well, you can't blame Lorenzo for wanting to cash in on all the noteriety," she said. "The obelisk is news."

"Thanks to you."

"And most of the newspapers around the world who picked up my stories."

". . . imprisoned within this solid granite, dear friends, and then bound with sturdy chains of . . ."

"We're going to have to leave before this final encore," reminded Harry, "to catch the last express to Paris."

"He'll be hurt."

"Not Lorenzo. Romance is more important to him than magic or— "

A polite tapping sounded on the door of their private box.

Harry stood and opened the door.

A red-coated young usher stood there with two pale envelopes in his gloved hand. "Herr Challenge?"

"Yep."

"Fraulein Barr?"

"As well."

"Cablegrams. Urgent. I am to remain in case of any replies."

"Thanks." Harry took the cables and gave the young man a half-gulden piece.

"Let's not open them just yet, Harry."

He shook his head, passed her message to her and opened his.

It was from his father and said:

> *Dear Son: You didn't do badly with the obelisk. Pack up at once and hightail it to London. Rich half-wit claims dead coming back to life and secret cult after him. Ought to be worth plenty. Your loving father, the Challenge International Detective Agency.*

Jennie finally pried her own envelope open and scanned the message. "Grand Duke Rupert has been assassinated in Bosnia," she said ruefully. "My darn paper wants me to get there right away and cover unfolding events."

Harry tapped his cable against his chin a few times and then returned it to its envelope. "Young man," he said to the usher, "you weren't able to find either Herr Challenge or Fraulein Barr."

"I wasn't? But you professed to be the—"

"All a mistake. Fact is, I'm near certain they've both left the country for parts unknown." He gave the cables back, along with three more coins. "You never will find them. Understand?"

The usher smiled. "Ah, but to be sure. An affair of the heart." He took his leave.

"Parts unknown?" inquired Jennie.

"Paris, actually," said Harry.

"I advise you, ladies and gentlemen," the Great Lorenzo was saying down on the stage, "to watch the next part most carefully. You will be absolutely amazed."